BUTTERFLIES IN AUTUMN

Charles Strong

Ajoyin Publishing, Inc.
PO Box 342
Three Rivers, MI 49093
1.888.273.4JOY
www.ajoyin.com

Butterflies In Autumn
ISBN: 978-1-60920-028-2
Printed in the United States of America
©2011 Charles Strong
All rights reserved

Cover artwork by Jennifer Doorn
Interior design by Ajoyin Publishing, Inc.

Library of Congress Cataloging-in-Publication Data

API
Ajoyin Publishing, Inc.
P.O. 342
Three Rivers, MI 49093
www.ajoyin.com

No part of this book may be reproduced or transmitted in any form or by any means, electronic or mechanical—including photocopying, recording, or by any information storage and retrieval system— without permission in writing from the publisher, except as provided by United States of America copyright law.

Please direct your inquiries to admin@ajoyin.com

CONTENTS

Chapter 1: I Can't Keep You Quiet   1

Chapter 2: It Ain't Right   17

Chapter 3: Honest man   25

Chapter 4: Righteous Lying   41

Chapter 5: Burnt Chicken and Bribes   51

Chapter 6: Innocence   67

Chapter 7: Injustice   85

Chapter 8: When We Get Home…   109

Epilogue   133

Preface

Every autumn the butterflies would come to our county. Pa used to say they would make a great migration from up North. When it became cold and too harsh for their kind, they'd fly down South where it's warmer. "Winter would kill them," he'd say. They'd spend only a few days in our county. Then they would have to be moving on again to keep ahead of the weather. Hundreds if not thousands of butterflies would flood our fields every year for just those couple of days. You wouldn't know when they would come, so you always had to keep an eye out or you'd miss the opportunity, which is true in a lot of ways in life, I suppose. Since there was no telling when they'd show, you always had to be ready.

Chapter 1: I can't keep you quiet

On some hot summer nights Pa would get restless. So to fix that, he'd go on the porch to his rocking chair and start to play his harmonica. A lot of times he'd play that thing long after dark. Sometimes I'd fall asleep listening to him play whatever tune came to his head. Well, one night in August I just couldn't sleep. I tossed and turned in my bed like I was on fire. Pa just sat there playing and rocking as usual. I became so frustrated from the heat that his music started to annoy me.

All of a sudden he stopped. At first I thought he had had enough for the night and was gonna' go to bed. I could hear him just fine from my room upstairs when his feet creaked on the floorboards. But they didn't move. I thought to myself, "Something must be going on here." Then he started talking to the darkness.

"Who's out there?" He waited for an answer. By now I was curious too, thinking he had heard a coyote or something. I got out of bed and peered through my window. Pa picked up a lamp next to him and lit it. "Who's out there? Come into the light where I can see you."

Nothing happened at first, then he said, "Don't be afraid." I thought he was saying it to himself. "Pa is a pretty strong man," I thought. "What does he have to be afraid of?" But then I came to the realization that he didn't say it to himself at all, 'cause out of the bushes appeared three bodies.

"Coloreds," I said quietly to myself. Two men and a boy about my age. What were they doing on our farm in the middle of the night? Why were they here? Did their master send them? If so, why were they being so secretive?

"What do you want? State your business," Pa barked at them. The two men looked at each other shyly. Then the smaller of the two spoke up. "Well, sir, we're looking for help."

"Help? What do you mean, help?"

The two men didn't know how to respond to that question. They just stood there with dumbfounded expressions on their faces. The boy continued to stand still like a statue. I guess he thought nobody could see him even though he was standing beside the other two.

"Well, sir, I don't know what kind of help you can give. Just please…don't tell nobody we came here."

All of a sudden I understood why they acted the way they did. They were runaways. Mr. Navin said the State would pay a bounty of five dollars a head for each runaway slave captured and brought back to justice. "A fine price nowadays," I once heard him say, "when an honest man's daily wage is a quarter." There were times I used to pray to God that we could have more money come our way. Now here we were sitting on fifteen dollars. We were finally rich at last.

"How'd you get here?" Pa asked him. They mustn't have been any slaves Pa recognized. I couldn't see their faces too well to tell who they were neither. There weren't a lot of slaves around these parts anyway. I could count on one hand all the encounters I'd dealt with them, and all those came from deeper South anyways. I think it was because most people said, "This place is going North."

"Well, sir, we was in the woods when I asked the Lord which way should we go. He says, 'Look for the angel playing the harp.' So as we walked we all listened for music. And that's how we found you."

Pa's harmonica led them here. Pa just stood there a little confused. The three coloreds stood too, silent as stones. It was an uneasy silence, but it did make me forget about the heat. A fly landed on the back of my neck, so I swatted it. My movement made the boy blink. Then he turned his head and peered straight at me. I could tell in his eyes he was scared. At the slightest notion he could wet himself. I thought to myself, "Now that's strange. What does he have to be scared about anyway?"

"How many are you–is it just you three?" Pa asked.

"No, sir. There's me, my wife's brother here, my son, my wife, my mama, and my two daughters. S-S-Seven in all."

"Go into the barn–up in the loft."

"Yes, sir. Thank you, sir." At that they disappeared back into the bushes. Pa took the lantern inside. I could hear him thumping around in the kitchen. I kept a close eye outside for any signs of movement. I could hear rustling, but I couldn't see anything.

My mouth dropped open when I heard seven slaves. That was more money than I could count. We were surely going to be rich now. I started to think of all the things our family could get with that kind of money. Maybe a mule to help old Beatrice, or a new wagon, or some fine dressing clothes. As my mind wandered and my eyes searched outside in the darkness, I knocked over a glass picture frame on my bedside table. Kneeling down, I picked up the frame and searched out any pieces of glass I could see in the moonlight. Still thinking about what we could do with our newfound fortune, I didn't notice Pa standing at my bedroom doorway.

"Boy, what are you doing up?"

"I can't sleep. Besides, I heard you talking to those runaways out there…"

Before I could finish, he pointed his finger at me and gave me a stare that sent a chill down my spine. I tried to gulp but I couldn't do it, being more than a little scared and all.

"Not…one…word. You hear me. Not one word to anyone about what you've seen tonight. You understand."

"Yes, sir," was all I could get out.

He put his hand down and his face softened. He let out a sigh, then he hesitated like he wanted to explain something to me but didn't have time. Next he backed out of my doorway and downstairs again. I hurried to pick up more pieces, then put them back on my table before I jumped into bed. I lay there thinking Pa might come back and talk some more, but he didn't. Instead he went outside where I heard him walk to our barn. I started to get sleepy now to the point that I wondered if I had dreamt the whole thing. Finally I closed my eyes, and before I knew it, it was morning.

I got dressed, then went downstairs for breakfast like usual. Pa was at the table eating; Ma was at the stove cooking flapjacks. Little Nell took to making her rag doll dance all over the table.

"Morning, Jessie," Ma said as I stumbled up to the table. She placed a plate of flapjacks in front of me. "You were up awful late. Are you feeling alright, sweetie?"

"I couldn't sleep." As I said this, I thought Pa was gonna' look up from his plate to stare me down like he did last night. It didn't happen. Everybody else was at their own business being happy at what they were doing, but I started to eat, feeling a little heavy inside.

"What are you fixing to do today?" Ma asked me.

"Me and Billy Navin are fixing to go down to the

creek to go bullfrog hunting. If that's alright?" I said that last part not fully knowing why I asked it. Maybe it had been a little bit of fear from being scolded by Pa the night before. My cheeks almost turned red on account of embarrassment at the table. Then Pa looked up at me for a split second.

"I don't see why not," he said. "Supposing you finish your chores and mind what I told you last night."

"Yes, sir."

Then there came a knock at the door. Ma and Pa stopped and looked at each other in surprise. "It's Luke," my ma said.

Luke was a farmhand we would hire a couple times a week to help Pa with the heavy work. He'd known my family forever. Though some people turned him away because of his jitteriness and nervous motions, he did have a good heart.

"Jessie," Pa told me as he got up from the table, "go tell Luke I don't need his help today. Something's come up, I won't need him till next week." He hurried to the back room of our house.

I sat there a minute and tried to make sense of it all. Why was Pa acting so secretive and nervous? Was it because of the coloreds that came to our house last night? Why didn't he want to tell Luke to go away himself? What exactly was going on here?

"Well go on, Son, do what your father said. It's only Luke–he doesn't bite," Ma said reaffirmingly.

I got up and went to the front door, the one away

from the kitchen. Luke stood there with his hands in his pockets while he kicked the ground. He looked at the ground, then back at me, still shuffling the dirt back and forth with his feet. He was looking as lost as a stray dog. Pa always did say he was a bit wiry for almost being a full-fledged man and all.

"Morning, Jessie," he said. "Is your pa ready to get started?"

"No, Luke," I replied, "he says he don't need you today. Something's come up and he won't need you till next week."

I looked around the corner of my house, trying to get a good look at the barn. Luke stared in the same direction. I jerked my head back quick when I noticed him looking too.

"Jessie, you're full of it," he replied. "I know you're up to something. Now where's your ol' man so we can get to work?"

Before I could answer, Ma stepped to the door. "Oh good morning, Luke, how are you doing?"

"Just fine, ma'am. I'm just here waiting to see when Mr. McCallister is gonna' be ready is all."

"Yes, I'm sure you are. Listen, as Jessie explained something has come up with Mr. McCallister. He's so sick he can barely make it out of bed. I hope you understand we won't be needing your help today."

"But we were supposed to bring in hay today. If we wait much longer it'll be too close to the rainy side of fall."

"I'm well aware of that, Luke, an' so is he. Believe me, he's more disappointed than you are. How about I give you this five-cent piece to make it up to you, taking time to come out here for nothing an' all."

My mother handed Luke a nickel from her apron pocket. My eyes got wide. I would've had to do a list of chores as long as my arm for a five-cent piece, and this guy got one for doing nothing at all.

Luke looked at the nickel now in his hand. "Thanks, Mrs. McCallister." Then he walked up a few steps and rubbed me on top of my head. As he set off back down the road, he waved and hollered, "See you later, Jessie." He went away whistling to himself.

Inside the house, Nell was feeding her doll a flapjack. Pa was still in the back room gazing out the window toward the hay barn. I walked up behind him. I could tell immediately what he was thinking now–it was thick in the air.

"Luke always was a squirrelly fella', but at least he listens," Pa said, still intently looking out our window.

"What are you gonna' do?" I asked.

"I don't know. Part of me wants to turn them in and be rid of this mess. Another part of me wants to let them go without any hassle."

"Mr. Navin says the State will pay five whole dollars a head for any runaways turned in."

"Thirty-five dollars is a lot of money," he responded, "but I wouldn't turn them in for the money. It is against the law to harbor runaway slaves. If I were gonna' turn them in, it would be so your ma and I wouldn't go to jail. On top of that, they might fine us or take away some of our land. We barely have enough to live on as it is."

Turning around, he got down to look me in the eye. "If I were to be put in jail, then we could lose the farm by the time I get out. Jessie, you're ten years old and smart as a whip. I know I can't keep you quiet, but you have to see the danger we could be in if somebody finds out."

"We wouldn't be in any danger if we outright turn them in," I responded.

With that Pa straightened back up, then looked out the window again. "Just leave that decision up to me, Son," he said somberly, "up to me and the Lord."

I left the room. It didn't make much sense to me. All I saw was a win-win situation. We could turn them in, collect the money, and they could go back home and stop living in the woods like animals. Plus we wouldn't get in trouble for keeping them in our loft anyway. What was Pa on the fence about when everybody made out okay?

Later that morning as I fed the chickens, Pa walked into the barn with a giant plate of flapjacks. I dumped the rest of their food on the ground and ran to the door so I could peek inside.

"How are you doing up there?" Pa hollered.

One of the colored's heads popped over a stack of baled hay. It turned out to be the same one that did all the talking last night. I guess he was the leader. He hurried over to the loft ladder and let himself down. Then he ran over and shook hands with Pa to the point where he almost dropped the plate.

"We're just fine, sir. Just fine, thanks to you," he said excitedly.

"Don't call me sir; my name is Jonathan," Pa told him.

"Well, Mr. Jonathan, sir," the man replied, almost stumbling over his words, "I can't tell you how much we appreciate ya'll letting us in like that last night. Especially for my wife, and mother, and kids. You are a blessing straight from the Lord."

"Well, bring them down here and ya'll can have something to eat."

"Yes, sir, Mr. Jonathan, sir." Then he made a hooting sound like an owl. One by one they all peeked out from behind hay bales, then slowly made their way down. They all appeared scared, like Pa was gonna' go shoot them or something. I didn't know why. I never heard of anybody killed over a flapjack before.

When his wife came down, she looked like she was hiding something under her dress, a watermelon or a bag of flour. Pa stared at her strangelike. She went over to him and took a flapjack.

"Ma'am, are you…"

"Yes, sir," she said, "about seven months."

"Has it been hard traveling?"

"Some days it feel like it gonna' bust out of me. At

times I pray to God for rest so bad that I don't care if they find us. But then…" She stopped talking and started getting all teary eyed. "I don't know what happen to us if they do. They was already fixing to take my babies I got now and…" She broke down. The man sat her down on a bale of hay and held her.

The other man came up to Pa. "Dhat's Sarah, my sister, an' her husban' Benjaman. I'm Rock. Dhat dhere is his mama, his two girls Gloria an' Ivy, an' Caleb his son, my nefew." With that he thumped his chest.

"Lord bless you, sir, Lord bless you!" Now the old woman came up, taking hold of Pa's hands in hers. "As I live and breathe I thought I was gonna' die on that trail before we got to freedom country."

"Freedom country?"

"C-C-C-Canada," Rock said, "d-d-dhat's wher' we goin." With that he shook his head and smacked himself a couple of times on the ear.

Canada? What was Canada? I knew of a few states in America, but not Canada. Wherever it was it must've been somewhere up North. Why did they wanna' go there, and why did they call it freedom country?

Right then their boy named Caleb spotted me. He raised his arm and pointed as fast as lightning. As he screeched, it sent the place into an uproar. All of them ran around in a panic looking for a place to hide. Pa had to put the flapjacks down and go to each one of them to calm them down. They were making too much noise to hear him, so he tried yanking some out of their hiding places. That just made them fight to stay down all the more. It was chaotic. The two girls were crying when they ran to their mama, and she was screaming, holding on to them for dear life. All three of them made one big slobbery mess. When Mr. Benjaman finally did come out, he went over to them, and he didn't know what to do to calm them down. One by one the rest of the family came to realize there was no danger. They all encircled the mother and girls to reassure them until it was peaceful again.

"Boy, get in here!" Pa thundered over all the commotion. I walked in with my head held low. I didn't mean to cause such a fuss. I felt so embarrassed. I stood next to Pa not knowing what he was gonna' do, but expecting the worst. He put his hand behind my back, then nudged me next to the family. "Benjaman, this here's my son Jessie. Jessie, this here's Mr. Benjaman."

I was kind of relieved, but still didn't know what to expect after he introduced us. I thought I was gonna' get a whopping just for showing up, for sure. Feeling a little more relaxed, I straightened up. The man bent down to look me in the eye, maybe to check to see if I was real or something.

"You gave us quite a scare," he told me as if I didn't know it already. Next he looked back at Pa . "I'm sorry for all this commotion, sir, Mr. Jonathan, sir. I-I promise we'll be good an' out of the way. Just please let us rest here for a spell till we're strong enough to go. You won't even know we is in here, I swear it."

"Alright, alright, calm down now, you hear. How long do you think that'll be before you're ready to be on the road?"

Unexpectedly the boy spoke up. "We don't take roads."

His pa shushed him, then kind of stammering he said, "Well, uh. Well, uh, what I meant to say, sir, is, uh, if you could give us three days, we would be mighty grateful. Three days to rest on account of the women and children and all."

Then he looked at Pa like a child, not knowing what answer to expect, just like I must've looked like going in there. Pa let out a sigh, then rubbed his forehead. When he looked up again, they all stared at him with that dumb expression on their faces, waiting for an answer. He glanced down at me; maybe I had it too because I was eager for what he was gonna' say. He closed his eyes, took in a breath, and let it out again.

"Alright, you can stay." Everyone's jaw dropped–including mine. Miz Sarah hugged her girls tightly together. They all reacted like they had won a prize or something. "Three days," Pa continued, "up in the loft. And you have to be quiet–or it's all our necks."

"Yes, sir, yes, sir, Mr. Jonathan, sir. You won't have no trouble with us. We'll be so quiet you won't even know we're here, no, sir." The man grabbed Pa's hand again to shake it. Pa started walking toward the door with him still attached. He was all smiles from ear to ear. I wondered why was he so happy. It was only a barn. It was only a loft. They still didn't have any beds, or blankets, or clothes, or furniture.

He kept on shaking Pa's hand till they came to the open door. Then he stopped where the sunlight started pouring in. He must've been startled by something, 'cause he just froze there and stared outside. He looked like he might've seen a ghost. Not even out of the barn yet, and he started backing up. Back in the darkness he finally let go of Pa's hand. As he walked backward, he waved. "Thank you, Mr. Jonathan, sir, thanks again."

I was taken aback by the whole experience. As Pa left for the house, I couldn't tell what he might have been thinking about. Then there I was, by myself, standing in a barn all full of coloreds. They all sat on the lower level eating flapjacks like they were going out of style. I almost thought that some of them were gonna' bite their hands. Each one of them took a turn looking at me while they were eating. After they looked at me, they looked at each other. I guess they were curious; I was curious too. I had never seen this many colored people together in all my life. In all my ten years I could've never imagined such a sight as this.

For some reason or another I started to feel a little uncomfortable. So I walked out of the barn. As I stepped through the doorway, the sunlight felt good on my face. I kept mulling the whole event over in my head. Halfway to the house the barn door closed, obviously from the inside, because I never closed it. I stood there and wondered. Now I had seen slaves in my lifetime twice before and both times they were in daylight and it didn't bother them any. Before I took another step I reasoned to myself that these ones must have been allergic to sunlight and that was why they traveled at night. But why didn't they like roads? Didn't they want to know where they were going?

I turned back to the house and started walking again. So many things just didn't make sense. Why did they want to leave their home anyway? Sure they were told what to do by somebody else, but Pa did that to me all the time. I didn't see any difference. And what did Miz. Sarah say was gonna' happen to her children? It shouldn't be all that bad unless they were gonna' put them in one of those workhouses–I mean after all they were just kids. What would be so bad as to make a slave try to run away?

Chapter 2: It ain't right

After I finished all my chores, I went bullfrog hunting with Billy Navin. Pa told me again that I could only go if I promised not to say anything. I promised him and I meant it. Besides, playing with Billy made me forget all the trouble of this morning anyway. About suppertime I headed back home with three fat bullfrogs in my bag. I only kept the biggest ones I caught because it just didn't feel right to keep the babies. Plus there were less of them to manage on the way home.

Billy always said that he didn't care. "They're all gonna' die someday." Sometimes he could sound pretty mean for no reason. I believe he got that from his pa. My pa never did take to him too much, but would talk to him on occasion to be sociable.

As I walked home, a butterfly fluttered past my head. I turned around quick hoping to spy more. My eyes went crazy searching in every direction. At last I sighed and realized in disappointment it was too early for them to come just yet. I got myself worked up over nothing. I turned around and walked myself home again with that single butterfly now getting out of sight.

"Soon," I told myself. After all, it was my most favorite time of the year. It would lead into harvest time, and then snow, and then Christmas. One year I missed them completely, and the rest of the year just didn't seem natural; it always felt like something was missing.

As soon as I got home I looked at the barn. I didn't know what to expect–signs of movement maybe. No noise, it was like they weren't even there. I thought perhaps they were already gone until I remembered that one fella' in the sunlight from this morning.

Part of me wanted to check. Another part wanted to leave them be, eat supper, and forget the whole thing. I guess the more curious side won out. Putting my bag of frogs down, I crept up to the barn real catlike. Next I pushed the door open gently so it didn't squeak. At first I couldn't see, 'cause my eyes weren't used to the darkness. I slipped in around the door and closed it a little, just leaving it open enough to find my way out again. My eyes still strained to see signs of life.

All of a sudden I heard scratching. Faint, not like any animal I ever heard before. I crept over to where the sound was coming from. I saw the boy, Caleb, standing off to the side kicking the floor with his feet. When I got real close to him, I said hey real whisperlike as not to scare him. It didn't work. He jumped nearly out of his skin and hid behind a beam.

"Are you alright? What's the matter with you?" I asked, but he didn't say anything. "It's alright, it's me, Jessie, from the house, remember."

He poked his head out from around the pole to see if I was telling the truth. "You scared me."

"I know I scared you, I didn't mean to. Ya'll is jumpy critters."

He came out, I guess not knowing how to take what I said. "We have to be on edge–not knowing who to trust and all."

"Well, you can trust me. Come on, I ain't gonna' bite you."

He sat down on a hay bale. I sat down next to him. We both kind of looked each other over, not knowing what to say at first. I wanted to ask him, "You got any friends? What's it like being colored? How far did you come from? How will you know when you get to Canada? What's ya'll gonna' do when you get there? You got any relatives up there?" And a whole bunch of other things–but instead the first words that came out of my mouth were, "So how come ya'll hate sunlight?"

He looked at me funny, like I was speaking another language or something. His eyes got all big and his head backed away. I felt a little embarrassed. Maybe it was something I wasn't supposed to mention. My cheeks started getting all red sitting there in the dark. Thank God he couldn't see it.

"We don't hate sunlight," he replied, "we hide in the

dark so no one can see us."

"Sorry," I responded back. I hung my head a little. His answer did make sense, after all they were runaways. "I didn't know. I didn't mean to offend you." He kind of relaxed a little bit after that. "You have any kin over in Canada?"

"No," he shook his head.

"Why ya'll wanna' go there?"

"It's freedom country, the land of opportunity. Everybody's free in Canada, no matter what color you are," he stated proudly.

"How do you know when you get there?"

"I don't know," he said, slouching. "Pa says it's up North. Way up North. Farther than we been so far."

We both just looked down, not really knowing what to say after that. Each one of us bounced our feet off the bale we were sitting on. I wanted to open my mouth, but I didn't want to look stupid or feel embarrassed again. My feet didn't know to leave, so I just sat there thinking of more things I could say, but probably shouldn't. Then Caleb chimed in, "How long you been white?"

"What?" I said, acting the same way he did. "What do you mean?"

"I heard tell that some people ain't really white. They is just colored people bleached. I figured if anyone was gonna' help us out there on our way, it's gonna' be one of them."

I tried not to laugh, but it snorted outta' me. He

was looking at me and I didn't know what was gonna' happen, if he was gonna' cry or get all red in the face. But instead he ended up doing the same as me. Finally we both ended up laughing, sitting next to each other on that there bale of hay, so much that either one of us was bound to fall off.

We laughed until we heard a hooting sound from the top of the loft. We both stopped. Caleb stood up and hooted back. "That's Pa," he whispered to me.

"Caleb, what is you doing down there?" Mr. Benjaman poked his head out from over the rafters to us.

"Nothing. Just talking."

"We have to be quiet. Do you wanna' get us caught?" He shouted it in a whispering kind of way.

"No, sir," Caleb replied somberly.

"Boy, get up here." With that he pulled his head back into the loft. Caleb got up and walked to the loft ladder. As he started to climb, I got up to leave too.

About halfway up I told him, "Bye, Caleb."

He stopped, turned his head, and replied softly, "Bye, Jessie." Then he kept on climbing. I was almost to the door when Pa stepped in. We were both taken aback by each other.

"Oh, hello, Jessie. Go on now and wash up for supper." He had a covered basket in one hand and a saucer in the other hand. I smelled biscuits. Ma must've made some gravy to go with them.

I walked out of the door thinking to myself we were gonna' eat alright tonight, and so were they. I loved Ma's biscuits and gravy. Biscuits were good, but not as good if they didn't have gravy. Without Ma's gravy it wouldn't be complete– something would be missing, kind of like that butterfly I had seen. Butterflies were fine and all, but butterflies in autumn–now that was a treat.

That night after dark I was thinking about Caleb and his family. I went over to Pa; he was in the back room reading his Bible by the window looking over toward the barn. Every once in a while he'd look up from the table and look out the window. I guess he was thinking about them too.

I stood next to him beside the table. The flame in our oil lamp splashed around like a catfish trying to get off a line. He must've known I was there, I reckon. You know how sometimes you can just feel somebody there without even looking. It's not that they're breathing hard or you can smell them. You get this heavy pull...like the kind that makes apples fall off trees. I watched him read quietly, seeing his hands move over the lines. Then he'd take a look up, let out a deep breath, and kept going.

Being quiet like this gives you time to think. I imagined Caleb jumping behind that pole when I said hey, saying he hast to be on edge and not trusting anyone. It ain't right for no boy to have to live like that. His parents should've stayed where they were at. It wasn't fair of them to drag a nice boy like him into all this mess.

I looked out the window and saw my reflection in the darkened glass. I covered half the barn. Then I tried to put myself in Caleb's shoes. Being alone, nobody his age to play with, scared. I did feel mighty sorry for him.

"Pa," I asked, "where's Canada?"

"It's hundreds of miles from here."

Hundreds of miles! How would Caleb and those two girls make a journey that far away? And in the dark too. It didn't make any sense. Why not turn them in now and get it over with?

"Are you gonna' turn them in?" If he did that, then at least he wouldn't have to be afraid of going to jail. Even if we didn't get any money, Caleb would be home and safe–wouldn't he? We would keep our house, our farm, each other. It was still a win-win situation.

"I still don't know, Jessie. Seeing them and the shape they're in, and listening to their stories just tears my heart. Especially that woman in there–seven months pregnant and all. Turning them in might be a punishment worse than death."

"What do you mean?"

He turned around and looked at me eye-to-eye. Then he placed his hands on my shoulders.

"Look, Jessie. I try my best to bring you up right. Some things I've taught you in life you've learned, made good decisions on, and grown as a person. But," he continued with a more sorrowful expression on his face, "there are some things in this life I've withheld from teaching you on purpose. I've sheltered you from some pretty rotten things that go on in this world in hopes that you wouldn't be corrupted by them. Listen to me very carefully when I say…a slave's life is a cursed life. There ain't no greater hell on earth than being a slave. You understand?"

"If that's the case, why would you wanna' go turn them in for?"

"I said the only reason I would ever turn any slave in is to protect our family. That's all, nothing else."

"Well, if slavery's so bad, then why do we have it here in America?"

He took his hands off of me and sighed. "I don't know, Son. I don't know. Only God knows why, but I don't know."

"Jessie," Ma called from outside the room, "time for bed." Pa looked at me like he wanted to say more, but the words couldn't come out. "Jessie," she called again.

"Go on," he whispered. Slowly I stepped backward. He turned around and hunched over his Bible again. I couldn't speak now even if I wanted to. My feet felt like buckets of sand going up those stairs. Halfway up I took one last look at Pa. His head chased his hand across the page, line for line, word for word. Then he looked up. The flame from the lamp still flickered; I could still see his face in the darkened glass. About now I couldn't tell if he was looking for answers in God's Book, or if he was looking at himself in the mirror.

Chapter 3: Honest man

Ma settled me into bed. I was all confused as she tucked my quilt down all around me. I lay there with a blank look on my face and a burning in my heart. Finally I ended up asking, "Ma, pregnant means having a baby, right?"

"That's right, Son," she answered, looking at me, half wondering why I'd bring such a thing up.

"So that slave woman is gonna' have a baby, just like four years ago when you had Nell."

She stopped completely and stared. Standing up tall, she asked, "What are you getting at, Jessie?"

"Well–what if she has the baby on the road? What then?" I said it like that even though I remembered Caleb saying they don't take roads. I just couldn't think of another way to put it, that's all.

Ma sat on the bed next to me. I was lying on my back looking at her. She must've seen some sort of worry on me, because she took her hand and stroked my face.

"I'm sure they'll manage, Son, they got to."

"But what if something happens to her on the way? What if she can't walk no more? What if she gets hurt, will she lose the baby?"

"Jessie, as long as that baby is in its mama's tummy, it'll be fine. Though stress does put a lot on a woman, she should be able to rest every time she needs too, like right now."

I don't know why, but I didn't half believe her. Maybe she believed it. Or maybe she just told it to me like that because she thought I was still a kid when I was on the verge of manhood. My eyes scrunched down, not knowing what to believe. My look must've caught her off guard. She didn't know how to take it so she became flustered. Then she asked, "Jessie, can I tell you a secret?"

"What is it?" Forgetting my confusion for a moment, I leaned in toward her.

"I also am pregnant."

My eyes popped out of my head. Of all the surprises that had come to me today, this was the most unexpected. "You are for real?" I was more than a little shocked.

"Um-hum," she nodded affirmingly.

"How do you know? When's it gonna' come?" I stammered as I talked while Ma leaned back.

"Oh, I just know–it's been about three months, not nearly enough to show yet on the outside. The baby will come around February next year."

"Does anybody else know besides me?"

"Only Pa, so now that makes three of us. You promise not to tell anybody until I show, okay?"

"Uh-ha," I agreed. I had learned from past experience when Ma was pregnant with Nell that you don't know if a baby's a boy or girl until it comes out. I hoped it was a boy. I prayed to God so hard last time that it would've been a boy so I could have a little brother to play with. I hoped he was listening to me this time. Having a sister is nice and all, but there ain't nothing like having a little brother. George Davidson told me that it was like having your best friend live with you all year 'round. Well, at least when they weren't fighting with each other anyway. But he did say it one time…I think.

"Ma, what'll happen to Miz Sarah's baby if Pa turns the family in?"

She sat back for a moment. She appeared like she wanted to say things but she didn't know how to word them. Maybe she wanted to explain it like I was a kid, maybe explain it like I was a man. Finally she stated, "I don't know. Those that believe in slavery treat people like cattle or pieces of furniture. More like property than people. They could take the baby and sell it flat out, or they could wait until it's strong enough to work in the fields. Whatever the case, it's doomed from the start."

I must've had a pathetic look on my face, because Ma put her hand on the side of my head again to comfort me. "Don't worry now, hun'. Your pa is an honest man; I'm sure he'll do what's right. I have the strictest confidence he will not turn them in. They're gonna' make it to Canada just fine."

"Ma," I asked, "why do we have slavery?"

She took in a deep breath and let it out again. "I don't know that one either, Jessie. Maybe it's because some people don't know how to live by the Golden Rule."

"The Golden Rule," I said, saying it almost sounding like I had forgotten.

She seemed surprised. "You remember the Golden Rule."

"Sure I do. Always treat other people the way you want to be treated."

"That's right," she said affirmingly. "So if you don't want nobody to tease you?"

"Don't tease them," I fired back.

"And if you don't want anybody to hit you?"

"Don't hit them!"

"And if you want people to be nice to you?"

"Be nice to them!"

"And if you want people to love you?"

"Love them!" When I said that, she dived in and wiggled her nose against mine. We both giggled at that. I still liked it when she did that–even though I was ten and all.

"Remember, living out the Golden Rule is a powerful choice and responsibility." She got up from my bed.

"Ya'll better now?"

"Yes, ma'am," I told her. She turned to leave, but as she was walking out the door I called out, "Ma." She looked back at me again. "I don't think I need you tucking me in no more."

She put her hands on her hips. "But I like tucking you in."

"You still got Nell," I reminded her.

Slowly she let her arms hang again at their sides. It seemed a little odd, but perhaps she realized something. "Oh, all right, if you insist. Good night." Once again she turned and continued out the door.

"Good night," I hollered back as she left my room.

I lay there alone with my thoughts. Colored people in slavery, secrets to keep, where in the world was Canada…I had had a full day. Not to mention Ma going to have a baby coming on top of it all. My stomach began churning along with the swirling tornado in my head. It sure was a lot for someone to handle. It seemed like there were no answers etched in stone anymore. I just wished life was a lot simpler again, like when I was Nell's age.

I didn't sleep good that night. I tossed and turned; it never felt like I had any rest until the rooster crowed. I couldn't help thinking about Caleb and his family. I wondered, what did it really mean to be a slave? Was it really as bad as Pa said, "Hell on earth," or Ma saying people were treated like property? That would be enough reason to run somebody off, I reckon.

Caleb and his family were good people; I hoped they would make it to Canada okay. But what about Pa? If slavery was as bad as he said it was–could jail be any worse? Although the State might take our house or land away, we'd still be free. We just might be able to start over. That made me remember something Caleb said yesterday about Canada being the land of opportunity. Now I'm not real sure, but I think that's what people used to say about America. I didn't know, maybe it had changed. If we did lose everything, maybe we could start all over again in Canada same as Caleb's family.

I stumbled downstairs. Pa was done with breakfast, Nell was in the back room playing, and Ma was still cooking. It must've been a lot of work for Ma cooking for another family and being pregnant and all. I looked in her skillet–there must've been fifteen eggs in there. I heard Pa tell her that tonight we were gonna' have to set aside two or three hens. "Who knows when's the last time they had a decent meal," he added. I knew right then and there that I would have some plucking ahead of me.

Eating that much chicken would have to be a carefully managed process. We were already using all the spare eggs we could find; now we were gonna' have to sacrifice more chickens. Less hens meant less eggs, not only less eggs for us to eat but also less chickens to be hatched. Then I thought about Caleb and his family sleeping at the top of our barn. I didn't know why I started beginning to feel selfish, maybe it was the lack of sleep. Here they were with nothing, and I was willing to pick a fight in my head over a couple of chickens. I should've slapped myself for being that stingy. Thank God I never said any of that nonsense out loud.

"Morning, Jessie," Ma chimed, "you're up late again."

"I couldn't sleep…again."

"Try not to make a habit of it." Pa interrupted as if nothing was out of the ordinary nowadays.

As I rubbed the sleep from my eyes, Ma set a plate of eggs, toast, and grits in front of me. My fingers stumbled over my fork as I reached for it. I caught a glimpse of Pa staring at me. I think he was either confused or embarrassed over me this morning. When you are the son of a farmer, you learn to make do with as little sleep as possible. But this exhaustion was becoming too much, especially since it was due to our new living situation. Luckily I got my first scoop of eggs into my mouth without a hitch. Maybe Pa thought I was funny; I just couldn't tell with him being all fuzzy and whatnot.

All of a sudden there was a knock on the front door. Pa grabbed the skillet. "Go see who it is," he told Ma. She wiped her hands on her apron as she marched to the door. Pa arched himself the way of the back room to try to see out the window.

In a voice loud enough for everyone to hear, Ma said, "Oh hi, Luke, what brings you here today?"

My ears perked up as I kind of heard him say, "Good morning, Mrs. McCallister, I'm here to see if ya'll need any work done today."

"No, I'm afraid not, Luke. Mr. McCallister is still sick in bed. He won't nearly have enough strength to bring in hay this week. And Jessie has been filling in with the extra chores. So check back with us next week, okay? If Jonathan gets better any sooner we'll come and find you."

"Yes, ma'am, I sure hope he gets to feeling better real soon. Goodbye."

The screen door slammed and Ma made her way back to the kitchen. Pa was doing his best to get a view of the barn, so much so that his arm holding the skillet didn't even have the pan touching the stove. Ma grabbed a hot pad and took the handle of the skillet away from Pa. With himself released, Pa dashed straight for the back room window.

After a few tense moments of silence, he came back to us. "That crazy boy is gonna' get us in a heap of trouble if he keeps poking his nose around here like that," my father grumbled to my mother.

"Now I'm sure he doesn't intend to pry, he's just…"

"We can't take the chance, Anne," he barked. "We gotta' keep him busy for the next couple of days."

"How are we gonna' do that?"

They started whispering back and forth. I'd had enough breakfast for now so I got up and left. I headed on to the back room, then looked out the window myself. Nell was still playing by herself, undisturbed by all the drama.

"Hey, Nell," I said to her.

"Heeeyyyy!" she sang joyfully back to me, smiling with every tooth she had. Then she went on with having her rag doll tea party.

I glared out the window. Peace and quiet–as it should've been. A few chickens made noise over in the coop, but nobody sticking their nose where it didn't belong. I wondered to myself, "What would the situation look like if somebody did find out?" Would they come and take them real quietlike in the dead of night? Or would there be a mob of folks raising a ruckus dragging out their family and mine as well? What about Nell? Would a mob have any sympathy on a child who didn't know nothing about the circumstances? Even if Pa did turn them in, would there be any guarantee we would all be safe afterward? They might find fault in us since we held them for two days before we told anybody. The State said to turn in any runaway slaves, but what if we didn't turn them in fast enough to their liking? We might have to suffer just as Caleb's family would anyhow even if we did the "right thing."

Pa's footsteps were heavy coming into the back room. He put his hand on my shoulder. "Come along, Jessie, let's go to the barn. Then we'll hook up old Beatrice and go to town."

"Can I come too?" Nell inquired.

"No, little Nell, you have to stay here and mind your ma."

"But whhhyyy?" she asked real whiny.

"Because she's gonna' need your help is why. You gotta' special job to do." Pa stopped for a minute almost straining to come up with something. He took a look at Ma tiring away in the kitchen. Then he got down on his knees to face the girl. "Nell, can you keep a secret?"

"What is it?" she asked excitedly.

My only thought was "Ohhh nooo! Oh no no no!" My eyes got real big and my heart beat faster. You couldn't trust no little girl with a secret this big. She was bound to slip up and tell somebody. Our whole family would be at risk, if not now, then later down the road. It was a big enough responsibility for a young man such as myself, but not a baby just over three years old. I froze from shock; I couldn't move as I watched Pa kneel next to Nell and get real close to her face.

"Now when I tell you this you have to promise not to tell anyone else, okay?" he whispered.

"Not even Jessie?" she exclaimed. Now why in the world she would say something like that when I was in the same room with her, I'd never understand.

"Jessie knows, but it can't go outside of this family. You understand?"

She nodded her head. "What is it?" she whispered.

Pa looked back at Ma, then at Nell. I felt faint. I tried to swallow, but it felt like a watermelon was stuck in my throat. My mind was racing, thinking, "What are we gonna' do, what are we gonna' do, what are we gonna' do, don't tell her, don't tell her, don't tell her, don't tell her." Then he spoke up.

"Your ma is gonna' have a baby." Her mouth dropped open and her hands slapped against her cheeks. I could've peed myself right there.

"She is?" Nell exclaimed, almost too excited to talk.

"Uhm-hum," Pa nodded reaffirmingly. "And it's up to you to come up with as many names as you can think of."

Nell knew some about having babies due to living on a farm and all. What with chickens, and cows, and asking a ton of questions, it was hard to hide the truth from her. She was gonna' learn anyhow so why not teach her right, my parents agreed. She knew some about mothers carrying babies, not nearly as much as me, but some…I think.

"Is it a girl? I hope it's a girl!"

Pa smiled and told her, "Well, we won't know that till it gets here. So I need you to come up with boy and girl names. You tell Ma and she'll write them down. As many names as you can think of. Then Ma and I will think about all of them till the baby comes."

Nell sat up proud, puffed up her chest, and said, "Radishes!"

Pa took his hand and rubbed the top of her head. "Well, almost all of them. Come on, Jessie." He stood up and walked to the kitchen.

I was still in a little bit of shock, but instinctively I followed close behind. Ma handed Pa a plate full of scrambled eggs and me a saucer of grits. We headed out the kitchen door. Nell went to the window overlooking the barn in our back room. "Tomato!" she yelled to us.

"Good job, honey. Keep it up," Pa shouted back as we rushed to the barn.

Slowly we opened the barn door. We both went inside, then closed the door most of the way behind us. Pa cleared his throat, then called out, "Hoot, hoot." We waited, then he did it again. "Hoot, hoot."

"Hooooootttt," came a voice from the top of the loft. I believe it was the father, Mr. Benjaman. Heads started sprouting over bales of hay. Soon enough they all made their way down the loft ladder. All seven of them came to meet us on the hay barn floor.

"Good morning, good morning to you, Mr. Jonathan, sir." Pa put the eggs down on a bale to shake Mr. Benjaman's hand. "And thank ya'll ever so much for putting up with us again."

"Tain't nothing. How'd you sleep last night?"

"Like a rock." I spied out of the corner of my eye the big fellow looking up as if he heard something.

"And the women?"

"Oh, we're just fine," the mother said, hugging the old lady. "Best night's sleep I had in weeks," chirped the old one.

When I saw Caleb I went right over to him. "Hey, Caleb."

"Hey, Jessie." Caleb had a smile on his face practically from ear to ear. I didn't know why he was smiling. Maybe he had a good night's sleep, or maybe he remembered laughing on that bale of hay last evening.

Or maybe, just maybe now, he believed that in all this trouble he'd found a friend. I smiled back at him because I believed I had.

"How'd you sleep last night?" I asked him.

"I slept great. No fussing or stirring, real peaceful-like. Almost like we was in freedom country already."

"Here, I got something for you." I removed the cloth off the saucer. His eyes got real wide and his mouth opened.

"Grits! They're my favorite! That and collard greens. I love grits!" Caleb ran to his mother, Miz Sarah, and tugged on her arm. "Mom, Mom, we got grits without me even asking!"

She looked down at him and smiled. "That's great, honey."

Caleb leaned in closer to his mother and said something I don't know if anyone else was supposed to hear. "I like it here, Mama; I wish we could stay."

Her face changed like she was surprised to hear that come out of her child's mouth–more shock than embarrassment, I guess. She placed her hand on Caleb's back, then led him to a darker corner of the barn so they could talk more privately. I didn't know if anyone else heard him except the old lady, but she left well enough alone.

I walked up to her. "I didn't mean to get Caleb in trouble." I said it even though I didn't half know if I did do anything wrong.

"Noooo," she answered. "Lord noooo, child. You

and your family is good people. Aint' done nothing wrong by us."

"But why did Caleb's ma take him over there to scold him?"

"She ain't doing no such thing. She's just explaining how things are and how things are gonna' be if we don't get to Canada. She ain't punishing him, child, not on the road to freedom country." She stopped to swallow hard. "Besides," she continued, "this place is the holiest we've found besides church."

I looked at her oddly. "What do you mean, ma'am?"

"It's an answer to prayer. We been on that road from one full moon to the next. Tired, hungry, always looking over our shoulder, most times not knowing if we were coming or going. This here's a place of rest. We can finally have a chance to thank God for this opportunity at the chance to be free."

Then, hesitantly, she placed her hand on my shoulder. Maybe it was something she had never done before, or maybe it was something she had been taught to be afraid to do. I didn't have a problem with it. Then she said to me, "The Lord bless you, child. The Lord bless you and all your kin' till Judgment Day. And if we don't see you again in this life, we'll see you again in heaven."

"Thank you, ma'am." I was a little taken aback; however, I did believe her to be honest.

Caleb and his mother walked back to us. They were both looking up toward the roof. The old lady did it too. I looked up and saw Pa untying the rope to the chute window. It was something we had in a top corner of the hay barn for ventilation. If the hay got too hot, it could catch on fire. Our chute window was facing the wind for the breeze to keep the hay cool.

"I'm sorry I never thought of this yesterday. It didn't dawn on me till this morning."

"That's okay, Mr. Jonathan, sir, you really don't need to go to any more trouble on our account. We just…"

Mr. Benjaman kept on rambling, I guess not fully knowing what to expect next. Pa pulled on the rope and pulley system hooked up to our window. He raised the trap door near the roof. Sunlight and fresh air poured into the barn.

Mr. Benjaman and the others stood in awe. He walked to the patch of sunlight let in by the window. It seemed almost magical, him being drawn to the sunlight like that. Just like an old friend he hadn't seen in years takes some recognizing to do. He stood there under the patch with his eyes closed. Feeling the warmth on his face must've felt good after being in the dark for so long and all.

Some of the others joined him. Those that weren't next to Mr. Benjaman just stood where they were and stared. I could see some of them moving their mouths without talking. Maybe they were talking to themselves. Maybe they were praying. Who knows? All I knew, was in all my life I had never been in a place like they were right now, just to be thankful for a good night's sleep in a hay barn and sunlight without fear. I didn't know if I'd ever get there in my life, but I started to wonder… did I need to experience the hardships they had gone through in order to not take such common things for granted?

Mr Benjaman looked at Pa. "Thank you, Mr. Jonathan, sir. We'll be just fine." As I listened to him, there wasn't the sound of apprehension or stammering like before, not at all jittery like Luke's feet. Maybe the light had some healing ability on him. Maybe he realized he could trust us and relax.

When Pa climbed down, he patted me on the shoulder. I guess it was time to go. As I looked back at them, I realized to myself that I had never seen a sight such as this in all my young life. It was both beautiful and heart wrenching at the same time–still, I never wanted it to end.

We stomped through the gravel to the stall where Beatrice and the wagon were located. On the way I was sort of brought back to reality.

"Pa," I inquired.

"Yes, Son."

"If we go to town, then Luke might see us."

"That's what I'm hoping for, Son. That's what I'm hoping for."

Chapter 4: Righteous lying

We rode Beatrice and the wagon into town. Just before we got off and hooked Beatrice up at McGregor's store, Pa told me, "If you see Luke before I do, tell him I want to see him."

I thought to myself, "Why? Aren't you trying to hide from him?" I could've scratched my head at that, but I didn't have time. Out of the corner of my eye I saw Luke hanging out at the post office. He saw us right away and immediately came over.

"Mr. McCallister," he hollered as he was getting closer to us, "I thought you was sick!"

"Weelllll, it ain't all like my wife says it is. You know women, making a big fuss over nothing." He slapped a hand on Luke's shoulder. "Listen, Luke, I got a little job for you."

Just then someone slapped their hand on my shoulder from behind me. I jumped a little, then turned around. It was Billy Navin, my near-bestest friend.

"What's the matter, Jessie, did I scare you?" he asked.

"Maybe a little, but that's 'cause you snuck up on me is all."

"Come with me. I gotta' show you something." He pulled me into McGregor's. We zoomed in between the two aisles of the general store. "Look at this." He said it slow as if I wasn't paying attention.

There on the shelf sat the most beautiful pocketknife a boy could dream of. My eyes got real big and my mouth dropped open. The metal shone like pure silver; you'd almost think it was polished by God himself. It was one of the most fantastic displays of workmanship I had ever seen in my whole life. "Whoa," was the only thing I could say.

"This here knife must be imported," Billy claimed. "Like from China, or France, or Montana, someplace like that."

It was a fine knife indeed. I bet a boy could cut down a whole world of trees with that knife. Wouldn't need an axe at all. And I bet he could whittle down a stick right to the piece he wanted with just one slice. Billy and I took the knife to Mr. McGregor's counter.

"Mr. McGregor, how much for this knife?" Billy handed the man the knife. He fixed his glasses over his eyes, then squinted. The anticipation was almost unbearable. I squeezed my hands into fists at my side on account of I was about ready to bust.

"One dollar and ten cents," he told us, handing the blade back to Billy and me.

Our mouths hit the floor. "A dollar and ten cents," we both said at the same time.

"Yep, see it's imported." He showed Billy the markings on the knife. I was too distraught to care. The two of us left the knife on his counter and walked out. Our heads hung low from discouragment. "Come back again, anytime," he called.

"A dollar and ten cents, who needs that stupid old knife anyway." Billy said when we were outside the store. "Why we could buy a whole mess of things with a one dollar and ten cents."

Billy said all this, but I knew him better. He was just mad because he couldn't have it was all. I would've been mad too except I was still in shock of the price and too tired from the lack of sleep, from the night before.

All of a sudden I got an idea out of nowhere. "Why don't Pa turn in one of those slaves living in our hay barn so I can get that knife." I slapped my hand over my mouth real fast as if I had said it out loud. Billy gazed at me real queerlike.

"Are you okay?"

"Yeah, I didn't get a lot of sleep last night and I've been acting funny." I told him that thinking it sounded pretty good, hiding my real answer. It was half true anyway. I felt nervous not knowing if he'd buy it.

"That's alright, you can just get some extra sleep tonight and be better tomorrow morning."

"That's a pretty good idea," I said because it was a

pretty good idea.

Along came Luke and the two of us bumped into him. "What's up with you?" I said, but I really thought I was thinking it to myself.

"What's up? What's up? Hasn't your dad told you what's up?" he responded. "What's up is your dad just asked me to go to Shiloh. And while I'm there he wants me to get some estimates on new plowing and farm equipment. That's what's up." He stood up straight, then looked off into the distance. "He must really think a lot of me to handle such an important responsibility."

"Yeah', he does," I replied kind of sluggishly.

Then Luke put his hand on top of my head and roughed up my hair. I always hated it when he did that. He did it every time he saw me. I shooed his hand away. Every time I told Ma, she'd say he was just playing with me, 'cause he liked me.

Pa stepped out of McGregor's store. I never even knew he was in there. "Come on, Jessie, let's go. I have a pretty good idea of what we might need now. We can come back later."

He untied the horse, then hopped in the wagon. "Luke, now remember, only the best, but don't waste time being too choosy. If you have to search out every spare piece of equipment in Shiloh county, so be it. Write down what you think are the best estimates on the supplies I told you I need. Hand over the list of estimates and sellers to me in a couple of days. I'll pay you for your trouble when you get back."

"Yes, sir, it won't be no trouble, Mr. McCallister. I'll do you right."

"I know you will, son, I know you will."

Just as Pa started to back up the cart, Billy's dad, Mr. Navin, walked up on us before anyone could notice.

"Morning, Jonathan, Jessie, Luke," he said as he walked right next to his son.

"Hey, Pa," Billy said to his father, "Jessie and me seen this really neat knife in McGregor's. But it's a dollar and ten cents."

"Well, I'll have to go in there and see this knife," he told Billy, "to see if it's worth my boy handling such an expensive piece of equipment." He then turned his attention back to my father. "Say, Jonathan, I hear tell there are some slaves running loose in these parts. You wouldn't happen to know anything about that, would you?"

Pa turned to Luke. "Luke, what are you standing around here for? You have to get ready for your trip."

Luke snapped back to attention. "Oh yeah, I plumb forgot I need to get ready. I'll see you in a couple of days, Mr. McCallister."

All four of us watched Luke walk off waving. Then Mr. Navin, Billy, and myself turned our attention toward Pa. I wondered what he was gonna' say…I wondered if he knew.

"Where's he running off to?" Mr. Navin asked my father.

"I need him to do an errand for me in Shiloh."

Mr. Navin leaned in a little closer. "Well, Jonathan, have you heard anything?" It was almost creepy the way he was looking at us and us knowing what we knew.

"Nope, I haven't heard anything. In fact, this is the first I've heard about it."

"I'm not surprised," Mr. Navin continued, "you being such an honest man and keeping to yourself all the time. You don't get out much anyway." He put his hand on his chest almost proudlike. "I myself heard about it from three trackers coming into town just yesterday morning. They didn't say how many there were, but they did say they'd share the bounty with anyone who has information leading to their capture. Up to two dollars per head reward for the whereabouts of where they're hiding at. Not a bad price if I do say so myself. If you do know anything I'd be willing to split that in half with you."

I don't know if it was what he said or the way he said it that put a chill down my spine.

"No, sir, I can't say that I do. I'm getting ready for hay to come in and I got to get myself prepared."

"I understand." With that he leaned in even closer to us, then whispered so no one but the four of us could hear him. "I really don't care if these outsiders are offering three dollars a head. Just between you and me, I'd turn those Negroes in to the State myself and collect the whole bounty."

He stepped back and placed his hands on the insides of his open vest. Billy looked up at him with a mixed sense of awe and pride. Maybe he was smiling because he was proud of his father's craftiness and cunning charm. Did my friend really aspire to be like that someday? Pa appeared like he could break out in a sweat. I was sick to my stomach like I could throw up in my mouth any minute.

"Yes sirree," Billy's dad continued. "Them Negroes don't stand a chance out in the wild–away from their element and all. Sure they got a tough life, but the Lord can't bless everyone, now can he? Who knows, maybe he might let some of them walk the streets of gold in the sweet by-and-by–I mean after all somebody's gotta' clean the stalls in heaven–but for right now they're just dumb animals. They should accept their lot in life and get over this running away business."

Tom Navin stepped back. He was beaming with pride over what he had just said. I also suspect he was waiting for other people to jump up and give him praise for it, one of whom he believed was my father. I think I was starting to sweat from the pressure even though I tried not to show it. The man then stared at me and asked, "Jessie, are you okay?"

Before I could answer, Pa sat up straight and looked Billy's father in the eyes.

"Tom Navin…I know exactly where you're coming from."

With that, he tipped his hat at Pa and took his son into McGregor's. This left the two of us free space to leave. Pa backed up Beatrice and our wagon so we

47

could go home. The last thing I believed I heard Mr. Navin say before we went was, "I always knew I could count on McCallister. He always listens to reason."

I was awfully confused riding back. "Reason"–did my dad just agree with Mr. Navin? Did my pa now think colored people were not worth helping? Had he always believed that and was lying to me the rest of the time why he wouldn't turn the family in? If he did "know where Tom Navin was coming from," why would he even be nice to them in the first place? How do you explain giving them a place to sleep and food to eat? Was that like fatten' up a hen before you killed it, letting them let their guard down so they didn't suspect you were gonna' betray them? I was confused by my father's "kindness"; it didn't make any sense. Why not just run them off seeing since Billy's dad said they're gonna' get caught anyway? Why place our family in danger? Pa said slavery was "hell on earth"…did he agree with that kind of evil?

It was a long and quiet ride home. I must've worn my anxiety on my face because Pa spoke up. "You alright, Jessie?"

"I suppose," I responded even though I was lying.

He stopped the cart, then took in a deep breath and let it out again. "There's something troubling you, isn't there? Speak up, be honest with me."

"Weeeeellllll," I said, not knowing how to say it. He wanted me to be honest with him; however, I didn't know if he had been honest with me the whole time.

He closed his eyes, like he was thinking, then opened them again. "Is it what Billy's father said that disturbs you, or is it about what I said to Billy's father?"

"Yes, sir," I spoke kind of soft, not knowing how'd he react and all. "What did you mean?"

"Jessie, what do you think I meant when I told him, 'I know exactly where you're coming from'?"

"I don't know," I shrugged, "it sounded like you agreed with him."

"Son, that's not the case." He put his hand on my leg. I looked him in the eye apprehensively, but still gave him my undivided attention. "I said that to him because I believe Billy's dad would turn us in the very second he found out we were harboring runaways. It's not a lie to what we've been doing. To Tom Navin's ears, it sounded like I agreed with him. He's so full of himself I had to make it sound like that to keep us from trouble."

Pa got us moving again. "But, Pa, isn't Mr. Navin a Christian?"

"I haven't seen that man do one Christian thing my whole life. If he is, he'd prove it by his actions." Pa looked at me while he was driving the horse. "Now listen, Jessie, I know you and Billy are friends, but his father is a downright scoundrel." He turned his eyes back to the road. "You have to watch out for Tom Navin and all hypocrites just like him. They'd sell their own flesh and blood for a price."

As we kept going I didn't know if he was still talking to me, or himself. "Maybe it's my fault that you and Billy are so close. I protected you from some things but I willingly let this one slip by. I should've put my foot down the first chance, had I known you were trying to be friends with that man's son, but having Tom Navin as an enemy out in the open would make life powerfully difficult."

"Pa…is lying a sin?"

He took in a deep breath and let it out again. "Yes, Son, it is."

I thought about asking him, why did we need to lie about our condition? Why did we need to keep secrets? Was there such a thing as righteous lying? Let's just do what we were doing and who cares if anybody knew about it–but I already knew the answer to that. Besides, those questions would be something that Nell or a kid would say anyway.

"Pa, I hope God can forgive us for all these lies we've been telling about our situation."

"I hope so," he said to me. "I think he will, but I sure hope so all the same."

Chapter 5: Burnt chicken and bribes

We stayed quiet the rest of the way home. Ma was in the kitchen again, this time making cornbread. It seemed like she hadn't left the kitchen for two days, feeding us and the other family and all. Pa asked her how her morning went. She said Nell gave her a full page list of vegetables and made-up words but nothing out of the ordinary. Pa then told me to go out to the chicken coop and catch three hens.

I trudged to the stable for some rope. We kept it near the stump where Pa did the cutting. The ax was hidden up high so as little Nell couldn't play with it. On my way to the henhouse, I realized I forgot my gloves. "You can't catch chickens without leather gloves, not unless you want your hands pecked and scratched to pieces." At least that's what Ma always told me.

When I walked back from getting my gloves, I saw Ma and Pa busy talking through the window. I didn't give myself time to wonder what they might've been talking about, but I bet it was about Caleb and his family.

I wondered to myself what would happen if Mr. Navin found out about us hiding a slave family. Would he really turn us in, with me being his son's best friend and all? Did that kind of money drive someone to doing evil, or was it already in them to begin with? Who knows. Why did that scoundrel, as Pa put it, have to be my best friend's father? Was he one of those people that Ma said choose not to live by the Golden Rule? Would he have wanted somebody chasing him all night and day for a few dollars in reward?

At the henhouse I spied my first victim. She was an older hen, not sickly but tired. Yeah, she was a plump one alright. Yes, sir, she'd do just fine. I kept an eye out for another two that we needed, and the rooster. I saw two younger ones with feathers pulled out of the back of their necks. That meant they were weaker and being dominated by the other chickens. I might as well pick those ones and end their torment by the rest of the group.

Once I was in I ran down the big hen, then jumped on it. Using the rope, I strung its feet, then I dragged it toward the stump. It was flapping and carrying on a storm. I needed to tie it down real good so it couldn't get away.

On my way back for number two I saw Pa leave the house and go into the barn. What could he be doing now, I wondered. Could he be telling Mr. Benjaman and the others about Mr. Navin, or the trackers he said to have run into? Could Pa be explaining himself to them as he did to me on the way home? Was he telling them to get out now before it was too late?

Number two and number three took longer to catch. Though they were weaker than the other chickens by the coop's standards, they still were fast. And there was also the rooster to contend with. He was fighting me every chance he could because he believed I was stealing his property (when in fact it should've been the other way around). On one attempt with number three, she slipped out from under me. I was there lying in the dirt, fighting off the rooster for the hundredth time, when Pa hollered to me.

"You almost done in there?"

"Almost. I got two already!"

"Keep at it. I'll be back to cut them in a few minutes."

I picked up the rooster and threw it to a corner of the pen. Then with all the energy my tired ten-year-old body could muster, I ran down that chicken and secured it. A job well done, if I did say so myself.

A few minutes later I was at the washbasin outside the house. I cleaned off my face and wiped dirt and droppings off my overalls. When out of nowhere I heard it…

THUD!

Then there was the mad flapping of wings. I closed my eyes and just imagined one of those chickens there running around with its head cut off, the last race it would ever run, still tied to a stump. It calmed down just in time for me to hear another…

THUD!

The same noise, the same image played back in my head. Before I knew it, there it went again. THUD!

It was over. Three hens done lost their lives to give Caleb's family and mine a meal. As I looked down in the water, I couldn't help but see my own reflection. I didn't know if it was the ripples, the darkness in the tank, or both, but for a minute I didn't recognize myself. I knew it was me but I didn't see me, not entirely anyway.

Then the thought occurred to me…how was I any different than these trackers Tom Navin spoke of? Here I was chasing after dumb animals for my own selfish means. Where would it get me? Where did it get them? Did that make me as much a monster as it did Billy's dad wanting to feed off of others in their weakness?

Dwelling on that any longer could've made my stomach turn, but instead Pa found me with three dead hens in his hands. "Jessie, I need you to get these birds plucked while I get some other chores done around here." I must've gave him a look that said, "Do I have to," because he added, "Come on Boy, do you wanna' eat tonight?"

I did it out of obedience rather than willingness. So I sat there pulling feathers out one by one. The clean ones went in one bucket, the bloody ones in another. All the feathers got made into pillows, coats, blankets, and such. The dirty ones just had to be washed better and let dry was all. One chicken was time-consuming enough–three was gonna' take me all day.

Then an idea hit me. Caleb could help me out. I put a chicken in each bucket and one under my arm and trudged off toward the barn. Opening the door as quiet as I could, I was moved by what I saw.

It seemed like almost the entire family was down on the lower level. Caleb's sisters were dancing and chasing each other in the sunlit patch. Rock was there and so was the old lady. The big man spied me and called out, "Caleb, dhat boy is here." Caleb came running up to me smiling, but out of the corner of my eye I saw his uncle thump his chest. I didn't have time to wonder about it though, 'cause Caleb almost tackled me.

"Hey, Jessie."

"Hey, Caleb," I smiled back.

"What you got there?"

"Chickens. They need to be plucked. Can you help me?"

"Sure," he exclaimed and we both walked to a bale of hay and sat down.

I set the buckets between us. "The clean feathers go in this bucket, the dirty ones in the other." Then we got to work. The two of us stayed quiet and busy. I don't know how much time passed before I spoke up. "Where are your folks?"

"Up in the loft. I guess Pa needed some time to

himself an' Ma went with him."

We kept working. Still in the corner of my eye, the big man caught my attention again. He was trying to say something to the old lady. I couldn't hear what it was, but when he was done he hit himself on the side of the head. The old lady grabbed his hand away and kissed him on the side where he had just struck.

"Rock's your uncle, right?"

"Yep," Caleb answered.

"How come your uncle thumps his chest or hits his head when he talks?"

Caleb all but stopped; that caused me to stop too. He looked up, and as real as life itself, he told me, "One day his master got so mad at him that he hit him on the side of the head and he fell asleep. When he woke up he had a scar, and he couldn't talk right no more. Short time after that his master sold him to ours for a fair price. Now when he talks and he gets it right he thumps his chest," Caleb thumped his chest, "saying, 'I did it.' But when he can't get the words to come out right, he smacks his head so they come out better next time."

When I took a better look, I noticed the side the man always smacked his head on was not the same side as his scar. We kept plucking away. I started to feel mighty embarrassed for asking that question. Even though I didn't do anything wrong to the man, I felt ashamed as though I did. I started to look down at the ground more and more; that's when I noticed something. Caleb didn't have any shoes on.

"Caleb, you ain't got any shoes!" I said it not thinking that he already knew.

He nodded his head. "I know it."

"Well, let me see your feet." I lifted my leg in the air and held the bottom of my foot in front of him. Luckily, and without complaint, he did the same thing. On the bottom of his feet were dozens of scratches and scars. Some gashes appeared fresh, as if ready to bleed at any second. "Did you walk all this way without any shoes on?"

"Yep," he said, nodding reassuringly.

"Wait right here. Keep working, but wait right here." I got up and ran out of the barn door. He probably had a big ol' puzzled look on his face, but I never stopped to check. Hitting the door, I thundered upstairs into my room.

Searching frantically, I went through my clothes dresser. My nicely folded garments were thrown everywhere. I didn't see what I wanted, so I looked under my bed. I reached deep under and pulled out a pair of fine, black leather shoes, Sunday dressing shoes (only to be worn on special occasions and such). Well, Caleb's foot looked about the same size as my boot and he was special alright. So I decided to give him my second pair of shoes.

Ma yelled from downstairs, "Jessie, be quiet up there. Nell is taking a nap!" I heard her, but I didn't care 'cause I was done already. I held my would-be gift in my hands and slowly walked to the barn. Wouldn't Caleb be surprised. I sure was glad to be able to give it to him. I sure was a fortunate man alive to own more than one pair of shoes so I could share with someone in need.

I got back in and Caleb was still plucking. I held the shoes behind my back as I walked up to him. "Caleb, I got a surprise for you," I said. Then I whipped them out with a great big grin on my face.

Caleb looked at the shoes with a longing. I believe he wanted to touch them, but he didn't. Then he nervously shook his head from side to side. And of all things he said, "No, I can't."

I was a little confused. "Why not? I'm giving them to you. Go on and take them."

He started inching away. "I can't 'cause of what Pa says."

I lost the smile from my face as I tried to figure this out. "What did he say?"

"He says shoes leave prints. On the ground people might see toe prints and think it's an animal and leave well enough alone. But if they see a boot track, then they know it's a person."

He put his head down and kept on working. With nothing else to say, I dropped the shoes and did the same thing. A few minutes passed in silence. Then Caleb said to me, "You know, it sure was nice of your pa to offer my pa those shoes he found at the store. Said it would take him some doing but he could find a way to buy some for our whole family." Then he paused and we looked eye-to-eye. "I ain't never seen my daddy cry before, but I think after that offer from your pa, he was gonna' burst."

After we finished plucking all three hens, I took them to Ma in the kitchen. I didn't know how she planned to cook all three birds at the same time, so I asked her. She said that was where I came in. Out back by the stable near the stump Pa had dug a little pit. I guess he did it in between chores while I was in the barn with Caleb. The pit had two Y-shaped sticks coming out of the ground on opposite sides. Another stick was on top of them with a makeshift handle attached, long enough to hold two chickens. We'd be able to cook one chicken inside and the other two outside on a spit, just like those pioneers did out West.

Ma kept the plump one in the house to dress it while I took the smaller two. Pa started a fire, then he stuck the pole through both birds. I had a box to sit on next to the handle to rotate the birds around so they cooked evenly. Pa left me to my work so he could finish his.

It was awful lonely there sitting all by myself. Ma and Nell were inside; Pa was doing who knows what. Caleb couldn't come out to visit me even if he wanted to; he had to stay hidden. So I just sat there, bored out of my mind. The only thing that kept me from falling asleep was that my shoulder pained me from spinning those chickens. Every time I peeked over at those birds they were still raw–not a hint of brown on them. I started to think this was never going to end. I was gonna' be stuck there turning those chickens forever.

"Boy, Jessie, you have enough food there to feed an army."

I spun around to see who said that, and my eyes nearly jumped out of my head. It was Luke.

"What are you doing here?" I replied all surprised and whatnot.

Then he stared at me kind of funny. I guess that wasn't the response he had expected from me. Was he trying to figure me out, or did he believe I was hiding something from him? "What do you mean by that?"

"Uhhh," I thought out loud. "Your trip, aren't you supposed to be going to Shiloh? My pa is counting on you."

"I'm already packed, but there's something I want to clarify with him before I leave. It's important and I don't wanna' forget by the time I get back. Where is he?" He started walking off.

"I don't know," I responded nervouslike. "Why don't you wait here, I'll go get him."

"No, that's okay. You're already busy."

Luke walked right up to the hay barn. I jumped up and ran after him. I wanted to shout for him to wait, but I didn't think of it in time. Plus I didn't want to cause a commotion anyway. He peeked his head inside. I grabbed the back of his shirt and yanked him out best I could.

He looked at me and his eyes were as big as dinner plates. His mouth dropped open like he'd seen a ghost. "What's you got in there?" He was talking like he was out of breath. He peered in again; I pulled him back as before. Then I put myself between him and the door.

I gazed in through a crack as quietly as I could. In the faint spell of sunlight, those two girls were drawing on the dirt floor. I didn't see anyone else in there except for their mama–as pregnant as ever. It was a miracle nobody ever heard us, or there might've been a commotion like the last one.

Luke spun me around, his eyes big. "Jessie, you got slaves in there. Are those the same ones that run away?"

I panicked inside my head. I couldn't come up with a lie to save my life, much less Caleb's family. If I told him I never knew they were in there, he might say, "You expect a person to believe that someone can have three colored people in their barn and not know it?" If I said we just had the three, he might ask where they come from and if they got separated from a family. I didn't even know where they came from– what was I supposed to tell him? Luke already knew we were not the kind of people to own slaves. We could barely get by as it was, much less afford a slave woman and two girls, no matter how little they might've cost. All these scenarios and ideas ran through my mind. The truth was gonna' have to be the only way out of this. I just hoped to God it was the right answer for all of us this time.

"Yes, they're the runaways," I told him somberly.

"How many of them are there? Is it just them or are there more?"

"Seven in all," I said without even thinking.

Luke rubbed the back of his head. Then he moved to the back of the barn. I followed him, wondering what he might do next. No one could see us as he paced back and forth, then he leaned down and looked me eye-to-eye.

"You got yourself a big problem in there. What are you gonna' do?"

"Pa doesn't know yet. If we let them go, we could all go to jail. If we turn them in, who knows what'll happen to them."

Luke stood up and started pacing again. I watched him anxiously, hanging on what he was going say next. Then he stopped and looked down at me as serious as all get-out.

"This is a mighty powerful secret ya'll have been keeping, isn't it."

I nodded my head yes at him. I could feel the sweat pouring down the side of my face. My heart was aching to jump out of my chest.

"Well, it's my secret now too. That means I'm in as much trouble as the rest of you if ya'll get caught."

"What are you getting at, Luke?"

He knelt down and stared me in the face. "If you get caught, you could come back and say I knew about the whole thing. Then they might take me to jail too. Sure you and Nell might go to a workhouse somewhere, but I don't wanna' go to jail. Unless of course…"

He stood up, still looking at me, and rubbed his chin. The suspense was almost too much to bear.

"Unless of course what?"

"Your family has the most to lose if ya'll get caught. There's no pressure on me to keep quiet…unless I had something that could keep me quiet."

He wanted a bribe. I started to think of all the things I could offer him. "Luke, I got a few marbles, a lucky rabbit's foot, a pocketknife, a…"

"No, no, no. What use does a man like me have for any of that junk? That's all kid's stuff." He waved his hands, shooing those ideas away as if they were bad smells. "What I want is some money."

My eyes got big again. "You want me to steal money from my parents?"

"No, don't steal it from your parents. This is between you and me. You've gotta' have some, don't you?'" I thought hard, then reluctantly nodded my head yes. "Well, go get it then and be quiet. You tell a living soul what you're doing and ya'll be sorry."

I sprang up and ran to the house. I used the door where Ma and Nell couldn't see me. Then I tiptoed up the stairs and made my way to my bedroom. It was still a mess from before. Opening my clothes drawer again, I gripped a tied-up sock I used as my bank. Clutching it like it was glass, I tiptoed back downstairs and out of the door once more. Then I made a beeline for the back of the barn where Luke was still waiting.

"Well, what's you got." He said it almost cockylike, holding his chin. I knelt down and opened it up. While I did this I was ashamed, angry, and scared all at once.

He sat on the ground to count it out. I had some silver, but most of it was in pennies. "Forty-six cents." He threw his hands up in the air. "This ain't near enough to keep a man quiet!"

"It's all I got."

"Wellll," he stood up and paced some more. "If it were a dollar that'd be something."

"But my dad trusts you," I replied, real agitated.

"Sure he does. After all, he is sending me off to Shiloh with an important responsibility." Then he stopped, and the look he gave me sent a chill down my spine. "Or maybe he's using it as a distraction to get rid of me."

"He treats you like a son." All of which was true. My father did highly respect Luke and pay him more than honest wages even if he was anxious and all. I had the feeling that Luke always felt that respect from him too, which might have been part of the reason why this awkward young man always hung around here all the time. At least that was what I thought he felt about my father before this particular moment in time anyway.

He knelt down again on the ground, picked up the money, then placed a hand on top of my head. "Well, being my brother, you'll understand where I'm coming from then." He rubbed my head. I felt so dirty I could've taken a bath right then and there.

He stood up straight, still looking down at me. "Now remember, little brother, don't tell a living soul about what happened between us here today. 'Cause first I'll deny it, second I might have to turn your family in. Now we wouldn't want that, now would we?"

I was so disgusted I couldn't say anything.

"Goodbye, Jessie," he said. "I'll see you when I get back from Shiloh. After all, I have to keep face with your dad and all."

Then he walked away whistling. I swear my chin really hit the floor after all this. We could've been brothers, but now he said he was off to betray me if I spoke up. After all my family did for him throughout the years, hiring him when most folks were just happy to laugh at him 'cause of his awkwardness, treating him like one of our own kin. He just proved himself to be no better than Tom Navin…a hypocrite and a backstabber. Why didn't I see this coming? I should tell my parents, but I was afraid that he'd turn us in if he found out, so I couldn't. This was by far the worst feeling I'd ever had in my life.

Pushing the screen door to the kitchen open, I walked up to Mama. I didn't know why, maybe it was 'cause I was numb inside and needed some comfort. I leaned my body against hers. I hurt, I wanted to cry but I couldn't. She said without looking down at me, "Jessie, how's the chicken coming along?"

All of a sudden I was knocked back into reality. Without saying a word I ran out the door to Beatrice's stable. Before I got there, I saw black smoke pouring from around the bend. I got to the fire pit, and the two chickens were as black as night. I kicked some dirt on the open fire to smother it.

Pa must've seen the smoke too. He came running from out of nowhere and yelled, "Jessie, what do you think you're doing!"

He spied me and the burnt chickens. He started to get all mad in the face. He threw his hat off and kicked it on the ground but didn't say anything. I slunk away from there while he was stomping. I didn't know how my situation could've gotten any worse than it was, but it did. I just ruined Caleb's family's dinner.

I sat down behind the stable and felt a hot tear stream down my cheek. I wished there were some rock I could crawl under. I sure wished I could take back the last twenty minutes of my life and do it over again. But I couldn't. I couldn't do anything right, I guess, when it came to protecting a runaway family.

Pa stormed over to me. "Boy, what's the matter with you? I ask you to do a simple task and you…"

I couldn't even look at him, my eyes were so runny. He wanted to yell some more but he didn't. His face was all red; his lips were fighting to hold in the words. Finally he just stomped out of there, leaving me alone in my shame.

Chapter 6: Innocence

When I had myself collected, I groveled back to the house. I didn't know what to expect, to get yelled at or a whipping, but at this point I didn't care. Upon reaching the house, I heard Ma and Pa arguing. I closed my eyes as I opened the screen door, expecting the worst.

Pa looked sternly at me even though I thought Ma had been talking him down some (at least I hoped). Still his voice was mighty angry. "Sit down!"

I sat at the table. He swung my chair toward him.

"I wanna' know something. Did you leave your post?"

"Yes, sir," I answered real mournful like.

"Did you mean to burn their food?" he asked even closer to my face.

"No, sir."

"Well, what are we gonna' do now, Jessie?" he asked standing straight up, still looking awfully fierce. "It's too late to get another bird and cook it."

"We'll give them our chicken," Ma chimed in. Both Pa and I looked at her; both of us were taken aback. "We'll give them our chicken. All of us can fill up on cornbread and milk. There, that settles it."

Pa threw his arms halfway in the air, then slapped them against his sides. "Okay. If that's what's gotta' be done, then let's do it." He walked off into a different room. "I hope one chicken will be enough to satisfy all of them."

"Did you mean to burn their dinner?" Ma asked when Pa was out of the way.

"No, ma'am, honest I didn't."

"Well, what's done is done. Now all we can do is just get over it and move on from here. But honestly, Jessie, try to be more careful next time."

"Yes, ma'am." I wanted to come clean to her, but I didn't know if it would've done any good now anyway. Threat or no threat from Luke, what was the point. Everyone was mad at me–Pa, Ma, even the chickens didn't like me. That was not to mention what Caleb and his family might say when we brought the family dinner tonight.

Later Pa and I walked the food over to the barn. He carried the roasting pan with the bird; I carried a mountain of cornbread on a plate. I was extra careful walking behind Pa just so my feet didn't trip over each other. As we got to the door, I could tell he was still mad about the whole ordeal. He stopped and without turning back he said, "Not one word about the burnt chicken." I nodded my head even though he couldn't see me. We went in.

We were inside the door and the sisters were after us. You would've thought it was their birthday the way they took to that cornbread. The old woman quieted them down, then took the plate from me with a "thank you."

Rock walked over to Pa. "Dhank ya kindly, sir, fo' feedin' us." He thumped his chest as he walked away. "I think Pa still wonders about that. I might have to tell him later when he's feeling better," I remarked to myself.

Mr. Benjaman and Miz Sarah walked up to us last, and she was crying again. I thought to myself, "Oh' Lord, I done it now. She must've known I came in here with three chickens and done burnt two of them up for sure. Because Lord knows it's hard to escape the smell of burnt chicken." There she was set off again. Hearing her cry ached my heart something awful. I didn't know how much lower I could get right about now. If they were gonna' yell at me, I wished they'd hurry up and get it over with.

She gazed at Pa, still sobbing and exclaimed, "Th-th-th-th-thank ya."

"Huh," I must've said it out loud 'cause some of those folks looked right at me queerlike.

"Thank you, Mr. McCallister," Mr. Benjaman spoke up. "Thank you for all you've done for us."

Then all of the family gathered around us. Each

one of them was saying things like, "Thank you, sir." "God bless you." "You are an inspiration." "The Lord will surely bless you and all your house." "Yes, thank you, Mr. Jonathan, sir."

"Ya'll never know how much this means to us," he continued. "Your family has shown us more kindness than anybody we've ever known."

"Except for the preacher that showed us about the Lord," the old lady replied. "No one else showed so much dignity and respect for this here family. Surely the love of the Lord is flowing through ya'll. When I was a young woman, still with my husband, the Lord spoke to me in a dream. He said, 'You are not gonna' leave this world till you are free, my child.'" She teared up and pounded her fist to her chest. "I believed him hard for many years. Even after they took my husband and my babies, I still believed. But I ain't never thought in a million years' time I'd ever meet someone like you. You are a light and inspiration for others to follow. If more people were like you, sir, on earth… think about how much closer we'd all be to heaven. God bless ya'll."

They all did it again. Pa and I stood there bewildered. They kept thanking us until we were out the door heading for the house. I wanted to tell them, "Stop it! I ain't so good. I did ya'll wrong. I burnt your dinner; we gave you ours instead. Besides, somebody knows about you being here. I couldn't even keep your secret safe. I'm a failure." But the words never did come out. It wasn't that I didn't like what they were saying, it was just I had already done enough today to embarrass myself–why add anything to it? I couldn't believe it all now even if I wanted to. Besides, I didn't want to insult them anyway. A chicken, shoes, sunlight, and a night's sleep in a hayloft, they sure were a grateful bunch. In fact, they were grateful for a lot of little things I had always taken for granted. I sure wish all of us could live more like that.

Inside Ma had the table ready. Nell was sitting in her chair; all four of us had bowls at our places. Pa and I sat down, and Ma scooped cornbread into everyone's bowls. Then she poured milk on her cornbread, next was Nell's, then she passed the jug to Pa, last was me.

It all remained pretty quiet until Nell called out, "What about chicken?"

"Plans have changed, Nell," Ma said. "We're not having chicken tonight, only cornbread."

"I want chicken!" my younger sister demanded.

I didn't know what to say. I hid my face as I spooned cornbread into my mouth. The milk ran down my chin onto my shirt. Now that I was back to reality again, I wanted to go hide somewhere. Then Pa spoke up. "The chicken got burned, Nell, what's done is done. Just be thankful for what you have in front of you."

Thankfully Nell stopped complaining and ate out of her bowl. Pa gave me a nod of confidence–it perked me up a little. I sat up straight and ate my meal like normal. Nell did not complain again the entire meal, thank goodness. In the eyes of a child Pa's word was the law. I guess that went the same for my world too.

Later in the evening after Nell was already in bed, the rest of us were in the back room. The grandfather clock struck nine. "Jessie, time for bed," Ma said to me.

I got up and went upstairs. When I reached my doorway, I stopped to look back to see if she was coming. "Good night," she called from below. Then I remembered how last night I asked her not to tuck me in anymore. I went into my room, leaving Ma doing some stitching, and Pa reading his Bible by the table near the backroom window.

After a few minutes, Ma got up and went outside. At first I figured she had to use the outhouse, but she didn't go that way. I could tell when I listened to the floorboards lying in bed. I got up to look out my window. Sure enough, she headed straight to the barn. I closed my eyes, then rested back in bed a few more minutes, hoping to go to sleep. It wasn't easy because my mind hadn't stopped racing ever since they arrived. Even though the night air was not nearly as hot as it was their first night with us, it seemed mighty stuffy to me for some reason. Next thing I knew I heard crying. I got up and took a gander over toward Nell's room, but it wasn't coming from there.

I slowly tiptoed my way to the top of the stairs. Now I ain't never seen my pa cry in all my ten years, but there he was stretched out over his book, weeping. He must've felt he was all alone before he decided to let himself go. I didn't know what to make of it, so I started to creep back to my room. All of a sudden I heard him cry out in a moan.

"God! Tell me. What am I supposed to do? Am I to turn this family of innocent people in, or help them on their way? Show me a sign, Lord…I need to believe. Please, Lord, show me a sign. So I know which way to go for sure."

I began to tear up myself. I thought he did already decide which way to go–him treating them so nice was how he done made up his mind. I guess he was still torn up too much about it. Maybe in his heart he didn't want to turn the family in, but he still feared people like Tom Navin would sniff us out. He didn't even know about Luke. Here we were living like sheep amongst wolves–no matter where we'd turn, somebody was gonna' bite us. I wished there weren't such hard decisions to make in life, that we could just do good and not worry about paying any consequences for it.

I lay in my bed staring up at the ceiling. Now there was one more reason I couldn't sleep that night. My head ached, my heart ached, my stomach felt queasy. It felt like I could be up all night again with this torment in my soul. I prayed to the Lord that he would answer Pa and be done with it. I closed my eyes in vain to give them some rest. Next thing I knew, it was morning.

Morning went on as usual…well, as usual as the last couple of days at least. Ma cooked more eggs and grits until we used up the last of each. The rest of us sat at the table eating. Some time went by when the thought occurred to me: Luke wasn't at the door begging for work.

Then my thoughts turned all sour. I was mad and scared at the same time. I glared at Pa across the table eating. I wanted to tell him Luke was a two-bit snake so bad that I could taste it. But I was even apprehensive of what he might've said, even though it wasn't my fault our secret was found out. I sure didn't want my family turned in, not after all we'd already been through. I decided it was best, for now, to keep my mouth shut about the situation.

We took the eggs and grits over to the barn. You know something, those two girls up and hugged me, one on each side. Luckily I didn't drop the eggs. Pa took the plate away after he got his hands free. It sure was nice of Caleb's younger sisters to hug me like that. They let go when Caleb came up to me.

"Hey, Jessie," he said excitedly.

"Hey, Caleb."

"You wanna' play?"

I started to open my mouth but Pa interrupted. "He can play with you right after he finishes doing his chores."

"Can I help?" Caleb asked. "It'll make them go faster."

"No, Son, you can't. You might be seen and we'd all get caught," Mr. Benjaman pointed out.

"Awww," Caleb started to say. "Ohh, all right."

Then Mr. Benjaman turned to Pa. "We heard that

there's men following us before we got here. That's why we don't take a chance at going out during the daytime."

"It's true, I heard that myself. I'll keep an eye out for any strangers that enter these parts," Pa assured him.

"Thank you, sir." Then they both shook on it.

"Call me Jonathan."

"Thank you, Mr. Jonathan, sir."

"No, sir, just Jonathan."

"Yes, sir."

Pa turned to me. "Jessie, let's get going now. We're burning daylight; those animals ain't gonna' feed themselves."

"Bye, Caleb," I said, backing away.

"Bye, Jessie. I'll be waiting for you."

The two of us walked out toward Beatrice's stable. As we left, I said without thinking, "Pa, has God answered your prayer yet?"

He was stunned. I guess he never did figure on me being able to hear him from upstairs. He took a moment to collect himself. Maybe because he didn't want to look, now how do those women put it, vulnerable.

"Not yet, Son, and if he has, I'm still trying to figure it out."

"Well, what are you gonna' do?"

We came to the stable entrance. He stopped, putting one hand on the doorway and one hand on me. This caused me to stop too. I guess maybe he wanted to make sure I was paying attention, so I looked up at him.

"I don't know. I want to let the family go 'cause it's the right thing to do. These are people, Son; they're not animals that you can sell off and forget about later. Don't you think the Lord cares about them too? They got the same blood running in their veins as you and me. They deserve a chance."

He closed his eyes, then took a deep breath. "My only fear and setback to this whole ordeal is getting caught. The consequences for breaking the law could be grave. Especially if information about our situation fell into the wrong hands."

"Like Mr. Navin–you said he might turn around and turn us in," I replied.

"That's right. Tom Navin probably knows if there is a bounty on people harboring runaways. But if we go around right now poking for details, that might draw suspicion back on us. We don't need anyone, Navin or otherwise, turning us in or having the government come down on us."

"We haven't been caught yet, so why worry?"

He looked at me more sternly this time. "This is nothing to play around with, Jessie. Even after they leave we gotta' keep this a secret. We don't wanna' do anything that puts our family in jeopardy. One slip could cost us everything."

I wasn't meaning to make light of our circumstances, just ease his mind was all. "Yes, sir, I know."

He eased up.

"If it wasn't for that I wouldn't care if they live with us all their days. They are people of character…and that should be respected." We continued on; it was good to hear Pa say that. Then he added, "I see that Caleb has taking a liking to you, Son."

"I reckon so. I like him too."

"That's good. His family are good people. I can't see why anybody would want to mistreat good folks like them."

I was out feeding chickens when who of all people should stop by: Billy Navin.

"Pssst," he said, "Jessie."

I looked over. "Hey, Billy."

"Come over here. I got something to show you."

I stopped feeding the chickens and walked over to the fence where he was. "What is it?"

Out of his back pocket he pulled out the knife. Yes, the knife, the very same knife we had seen back at McGregor's. My eyes got big like flapjacks. I could tell because I could see the reflection of my face on the knife itself.

"Whoa! How'd you get it?"

"My dad got it for me," he beamed proudly. "He talked Mr. McGregor down to ninety cents. Can you believe it! Ninety cents down from one dollar and ten cents, now that's a bargain!"

"How'd he do that?"

"My dad was arguing with Mr. McGregor forever.

Well, at least over an hour anyway, saying stuff like, 'Nobody with any sense around these parts would pay so much for a knife.' 'It's an overpriced piece of equipment that's just gonna' collect dust.' 'He might as well do himself a favor and unload it on us for a lesser price.' Well, after a time Mr. McGregor caved in. Isn't she a beauty?"

It was a nice knife, but I wondered how big a headache Billy's dad gave the store owner for it. They didn't have to buy that knife anyway. What would've been worth more to Mr. McGregor–to sell a knife, or get Mr. Navin off his back?

"You wanna' go down to the creek?" he asked, putting it back in his pocket.

I remembered my promise to Caleb. "I can't, I'm busy today."

"What's you gotta' do?"

"I got a whole mess of chores to do before we bring the hay in."

"Aw, come on, Jessie. A man's only a boy once in his life."

"Well, I'll have to ask Pa," I said, hoping to pass the buck.

"What'd you wanna' do that for? Just pick up and go. You can always come back later to finish up."

I walked out of the chicken pen, Billy following me. The two of us went together searching for my pa. Billy was nagging me all the way to just go–"He won't know nothing." Then he took a notion to look inside the hay barn. I changed his mind and we headed out toward the fields.

We found Pa in the middle of the field inspecting the hay that needed to be harvested. Billy ran up to him first, I trudged after.

"Good afternoon, Mr. McCallister. Do you mind if Jessie goes out to the creek with me today?" Next he put on a smile as if a halo was gonna' appear over his head. "Pleasssseeee."

Pa looked a little stunned as to why Billy was here. Then he looked at me. I hoped he could tell by my expression that all this wasn't my idea.

"Jessie can't right now, he's got chores to do."

"Awww, please, Mr. McCallister," he whined. Then he came up with a notion. "Well, if you want I can hang around here until he gets them all done. Maybe I could help him too."

I knew exactly what Pa was thinking, "NO!" He knew just as well as I did that Billy wouldn't lend a hand to help, not unless you directed him to do it. He also knew that once you gave him a job to do you had to stay on top of him. "Spoiled" I think was the term he liked to say about Billy. Not to mention our visitors living in the barn on top of everything. Pa took his hat off and scratched his head. Maybe he was thinking of the best way to tell him to leave without looking suspicious. I was waiting for Pa's answer, nearly holding my breath.

"I'll give you an hour," he stated. Billy jumped up

in the air; my jaw dropped. "One hour, Billy Navin, that's all. But if you ain't back here by then, I'll tell the marshal to take a switch to both of you and throw you in jail for the night. Jessie, remember what I told you, and also remember that those chores ain't gonna' keep forever."

"Yes, sir," Billy piped up. "Come on, Jessie, let's go."

As we walked away I looked back at Pa. He shrugged his shoulders and gave me a look that seemed to tell me, "What else can we do?" I knew Billy was my best friend and all, but he could be a real pest sometimes. Not to mention Pa not speaking too kindly about Mr. Navin the other day. I didn't wanna' go–but we all had to make sacrifices, I guess. If it would get Billy out of here, then that was one less headache for the rest of us. I couldn't afford another episode like the one yesterday with Luke.

"You see, Jessie," Billy remarked as we were walking off my farm down the road, "it's just like my dad always says. 'If you set your mind to something, just stick to the matter till the other person caves in. That's how you get what you want out of life.'"

Down at the creek we didn't do much of anything. Billy made a makeshift fishing pole from a stick, some twine, and a hook. He had all of it stuffed in his pockets from before he came to get me. It sat in between us. It wasn't a very impressive-looking pole, but it didn't matter. I just sat down to rest a spell. Billy whittled on every piece of wood he could find. The hour went by kind of lazily–I liked it. This was the most rested I'd felt in the last couple of days.

"What did your dad mean when he said, 'Remember what I told you'?" Billy spoke up, still working on a stick.

"Oh, it's nothing," I replied, trying to think of something quick. "Just a little family thing is all."

He stopped whittling and gazed at me. "What is it? Come on, Jessie, ain't you gonna' tell your best friend.? I promise I won't tell."

I didn't have to open my mouth a second time. For by some stroke of luck, or a miracle, the top of our fishing pole began to move. Billy put his whittling down as we both intently watched the top of the pole twitch. There we were eyeing that thing like two cats going after the same mouse.

Before I knew it we were both scrambling for that makeshift pole, each fighting to keep our hands on it. Both of us ended up on the ground, rolling side to side over top of each other, shouting.

"It's mine–give it back! I made it," Billy screamed.

"You got your knife! I didn't bring nothing else," I yelled back at him.

"That's not my fault!"

"Let me catch this one! You can have the next one!"

"There might not be a next one!"

"LET GO!"

"NO! YOU LET GO!"

"I GRABBED IT FIRST–NOW LET GO!"

"NO, YOU DIDN'T!"

We did so much whooping and hollering neither one of us saw where we were going. We both rolled right off the bank and into the water. Each of us sat up. The pole was nowhere to be found.

"Uhhhh!" I screamed in disappointment.

"You lost the pole!" Billy shouted at me.

"I didn't lose it. You lost it!"

"If you would've let go, we'd still have it!"

Then we stopped arguing and listened. The frogs were croaking up a storm because of the disturbance. That gave me an idea.

"Hey, Billy, why don't we go frog hunting instead. We're already wet, why not make the most of it."

That seemed to set well with him, so we were off. There the two of us went creeping along the edge of the bank till we came to a marshy part of the creek. I was keeping my eyes open for any signs of life to be seen in the thicket. Billy was behind me.

All of a sudden I heard a SPLASH! I took a look back and there was a disturbance in the water. Next thing I knew Billy popped up, shouting, "I got one!" I helped him out. He was all covered in muck and slime and stuff. We both took a look at his catch. It was a frog alright, a prizewinning bull. It might've been the biggest frog I'd seen in weeks. Billy sure was a lucky man to find a behemoth like that.

All of a sudden he started patting his pockets frantically. "What's wrong?" I asked.

"My knife. My knife. I think I lost my knife!"

"Did you lose it in the water?"

"No," Billy said stopping for a moment. "I think I know where it is."

He ran back to the tree where we were at before; I followed him. Billy had the frog by its legs in one hand. I watched it swing with the motion of his arms. It was kind of funny to watch, but I'd bet anything that frog wished he was somewhere else right now.

We both came to the tree we were resting at earlier. Billy got down on his hands and knees still holding onto his frog. There were scattered pieces of wood everywhere; I guess his knife must've gotten lost in our scuffle. He was searching the grass and under all the broken timber. I got down on the ground to help him look too.

Then I spied a tiny gleam of sunlight in the grass. I crawled over and there it was. As I picked up the knife, I could see my reflection from its handle to its blade. The wood barely tarnished it at all. It was still the shiniest, most beautiful knife a boy could ever dream to own.

"Hey, Billy, I found it."

"Oh, good," he said crawling over to me as fast as he could. "Thank you, Jessie."

He took the knife back with his free hand. The other one still had the frog by both its hind legs to the ground on its belly. Billy raised the arm with the knife over his head. Its blade was pointed down toward the captive frog. Without warning, Billy brought the blade down to earth on top of its helpless victim.

"What are you doing?" I yelled at him, but it was no use. Billy's eyes were bulging, his teeth clenched like he was in a rage. Blood went everywhere–on him, in the grass; some of it even got on me. He raised his fist as quick as lightning and brought it down just the same again. After five or six times you couldn't tell what the creature was anymore.

I stood up and backed away from him. As he looked at me, the crazed look in his eyes started to dim. His mouth eased back to normal. While he stared at me he asked, "What's the matter with you, Jessie?"

"What's the matter with me?" I responded, still trying to take the whole thing in. "What's the matter with you? You didn't have to go kill that frog."

"What do you think I do with the ones I catch, keep them as pets?" He wiped the blade on the grass, stood up, dropped the mess from his hand, then folded up the knife. While placing it back in his pocket, he took a few steps toward me. "Honestly, Jessie, you can't stay a child forever. You gotta' realize all these critters are gonna' die someday."

I gandered up at the sky to see where the sun was. "I reckon its time for me to get back home."

"I reckon," he said coldly and covered in blood. "Let's go."

Chapter 7: Injustice

As we started walking down the road, it was a quiet trip. I had always assumed Billy let his frogs go like I always did mine. I was shocked to say the least when I saw him switch so dramatically from my best friend one minute to frog-killing maniac the next. Maybe I was too naïve, I started to think as we continued onward. Billy's dad did say that coloreds were "dumb animals." Pa said "he ain't never seen his father do one Christian thing in his life," and that "Tom Navin would sell his own flesh and blood for a price." Perhaps some of this mean-spiritedness done rubbed off on his son. Perhaps he was so good at hiding it 'cause they were both so charming and all. Whatever the reason, this new side I had seen in my friend started to worry me.

I didn't have much time to think on it. Behind us was the sound of thundering hoofbeats. Billy and I turned around. Riding up to us were three men that I had never seen before. We backed off of the road to let them pass through, but instead they stopped their horses right in front of us.

All three men were wearing long, expensive coats and dark, brimmed hats. Each man had a rifle on one side of his horse and a revolver on the other. One horse was an Appaloosa. I didn't know much about horses, but I definitely knew an Appaloosa when I saw one, on account of that was the type Beatrice was. All three of them were rough-bearded and dirty, like they'd been riding for days.

"Morning, boys," one of them said to us.

"Hey, I know you," Billy replied back. "Ya'll are those trackers that spoke to my pa about hunting down Negroes in these parts."

"The same," he answered back.

"We'd like to know if either one of you two have seen or heard anything in the last couple of days concerning them. We'll make it worth your while," another one chimed in.

"How much?" Billy asked. I looked at him in bewilderment. Was this my friend talking to these men, or his father talking through him?

"One quarter per head," the man on the Appaloosa answered.

"Twenty-five cents," Billy replied indignantly. "You told my pa two dollars!"

"Twenty-five cents is nothing to sneeze at, boy," he remarked. "It's still a full day's wages to any hardworking man alive."

Billy didn't look like he believed them. "Why did you go and promise my pa two dollars and me only a quarter?"

"Who's your pa, son?" the third one asked. His voice was gruffer than the other two, like he'd been eating gravel or something.

"Tom Navin," Billy beamed proudly.

The three men looked at each other and whispered so Billy and I couldn't hear. My ears were itching to know what they were talking about, but I dared not get any closer. I was kind of nervous around them anyway. Billy didn't seem to have a problem. Maybe it was because he'd met them before, or maybe because I knew what I knew.

"Who are you?" The second man spoke, looking at me.

"I'm Billy Navin and this here's my good friend Jessie McCallister."

"Our apologies, Billy," the first man declared. He must've been the lead man for doing so much of the talking. "We didn't recognize you. Please know we hold the utmost respect for your father. We all know your dad is an important man, especially when it comes to the things that matter most."

"Like being loyal to the South," the second one added.

"After all, hiding fugitives is against the law in this state," the third one pointed out.

"What my companions are saying is, we weren't

sure about your friend here," the one on the Appaloosa continued, "if we can trust him."

"Don't worry about him," Billy said, putting his hand on my shoulder. "Him and his daddy are just fine."

"Good. Now that that's out of the way, can you give your pa a message?" The lead man looked my way. "Go home and tell your daddy that loyalty matters, and that loyalty to the South pays. Especially when it comes to keeping Negroes in their places."

"Now as for you, Billy," they turned their attention back toward him. "Go back and tell your daddy that leads are running soft. Because of this we have to drop our price to one dollar and fifty cents."

"But," the second one chimed in, "for his sake, and his sake only, we'll pay him cash up front upon their physical capture instead of waiting until they're properly turned in. Now remember, that's upon their capture."

"This would be better for him," the first one added. "We get our people, he gets his money up front instead of waiting. It could take weeks for him to get reimbursed by the State and all."

"Politics is a dirty business," the gruff one remarked. "But your dad understands that. After all–he is a lobbyist."

"Don't worry none about us," Billy stated while reaching in his back pocket. He opened his blade and quickly snapped it up as he proclaimed, "If I find any Negroes… I'll stick them."

The three men laughed at this. I guess they thought it was funny, but I didn't see any humor in it. What could be so funny about wanting to stab somebody? I looked at Billy with the blade he was holding defiantly. He was not laughing; in fact, the expression on his face was as serious as it could get. I looked at the blade. It was not near as shiny as when I held it before. It was all gray and dingy-looking. Even with no blood on it, the knife looked tainted, like it had been worn out and used over for all the wrong purposes.

"Now, now, son," the lead man said, calming himself down. "No need for that. This is man's work. A boy like yourself could get hurt. You just tell us where they're held up at and we'll take care of the rest."

"Thank you for your time, gentlemen." With that they trotted away. They went off still talking, but I couldn't hear what they were saying. Then the gruff one jerked his fist up just like Billy did holding his knife. They all laughed again until they were out of sight.

I looked again at Billy in amazement. He had put his knife away, then he started to walk back down the road as if nothing had happened. I was still in shock as I stood there until he finally waved me to come with him. I needed to jog to catch up.

"Billy, I thought your pa only grew tobacco. What's a lobbyist?" I asked, trying to cover up my confusion about the event I'd just seen.

"My pa says a lobbyist is someone who goes to the

State capitol and tells the politicians what to do. Pa says he just might be more powerful than any senator or governor put together. Can you imagine that!"

I was still taken aback by the whole encounter, so I didn't say anything else. It was quiet the rest of the way until we reached my house. Billy left, I went inside. Ma saw me and gasped.

"Go outside and get cleaned up this instant." I guess I plumb forgot about still having creek mud all over myself. She went to the kitchen to pump some water into a pail. When the pail was full she grabbed a rag, then came back to my trail of muddy footprints. "Take those clothes and boots and go outside with them. NOW!"

While Ma cleaned the floor, I dropped my dirty clothes on the porch. She was back there talking to herself, but I paid no heed. I went to the outside pump, the one we water our animals with, and filled the bin. I rinsed off everything, even the muck out of the bin. Now I was cold and wet standing outside in my long johns. At this particular time I realized I came out without a towel or dry change of clothes. So I walked back into the house in my sopping wet underwear. I entered through the kitchen and headed toward the stairs.

"Jessie! What are you doing to me?" I looked back where I came from. Now I saw a trail of water from the kitchen door to the very spot I was standing.

"Sorry, Ma," I squeaked out.

"Go on and get dressed!" I continued upward. Ma was still on the floor cleaning mud and talking to herself all the while.

After I was dressed I went downstairs. Now Ma was cleaning up the water on the kitchen floor. I asked her if she wanted me to help, but she was still frustrated 'cause she barked "NO!" I went outside with my good shoes on, the same ones I was gonna' give Caleb. I searched out Pa and found him feeding Beatrice.

"Good you're back. Finish your chores and don't spend all day playing with Caleb. We have a job to do later on tonight."

I plumb forgot about Caleb. I wanted to tell my father everything about the trackers and Billy, but instead my body immediately went right to work finishing what chores I was supposed to do. How am I gonna' tell him, I wondered? This wasn't the kind of threat like Luke's. "You tell anyone I know and I'll turn your family in." This threat was out in the open and as real as it could get, not just the fact that they were searching out Caleb's family, but also how they were in cohorts with the Navins. I guess I might not have been as much of a man as I thought I was, because this was a very stressful situation for a person to be under.

After I was done with my chores, I went inside the barn. No one seemed to be there in the open, so I hooted. Before I finished, Caleb popped his head up.

"Hey, Jessie. I've been waiting for you." I thought he'd be mad at me for taking so long but he wasn't. In fact, he was grinning from ear to ear when he saw me. I was glad; in fact, seeing him made my troubles just melt away.

He was still grinning as he climbed down the loft ladder. Then somehow the sleeve of his shirt got caught on a loose nail or something. As he moved toward me, his shirt nearly ripped in half.

He stood there looking at the thing. "Ohhh nooo!"

Somebody, I think his mama, called from the top of the loft, "What's the matter, Son?"

"My shirt's ripped. Can you fix it, Mama?"

"I don't have nothing to mend it with."

"What am I gonna' do?" he asked me. "This is my only shirt."

"Don't worry, Caleb, I'll take it to my ma. She might be able to fix it."

"That's a good idea, Son," his mama stated confidently. "And if she can't, then she can bring the stuff to me so I can."

Caleb took off the rest of his shirt. I ran it back to the house. Ma was sitting in a chair in the back room with Nell playing on the floor. I walked up to her cautiously 'cause I didn't know if she was still mad.

She looked up at me. "Yes–what is it now?"

I held the shirt in front of her and timidly asked, "Would you please fix this?"

"This isn't your shirt. Where did you get it?"

"No, ma'am." I held myself back from saying it was Caleb's shirt because Nell was close by. I guess I didn't need to, she kind of got the idea.

"Tell the owner of this shirt I'll do the best I can." As she looked it over, Nell walked up and grabbed it, thinking it'd be fun to play tug o' war with it. We both shooed her away. She sat back down. She must not have understood, 'cause she looked at us queer. To her it was just a rag; to Caleb it was the only shirt he owned. As I walked out to leave, Ma called back, "Jessie."

"Yes, ma'am."

"How many times have I told you not to drag mud on the floor?"

"A lot."

"Don't…do…it…again."

"Yes, ma'am." With that I left and ran back to the hay barn. I guess it was easy for a boy like myself to forget how a dirty floor could make women awful angry.

Back in the barn Caleb was going around a support beam, dragging his hand along behind him. The sunlight was hitting the side of the beam that faced the door. He kept spinning around the pole as I approached him; then I noticed something peculiar about his back.

"Hey, Caleb, stop and turn around." He did, and to my amazement every square inch of his back was covered in long, ugly scars. My jaw dropped open. "What happened to you?"

"What do you mean?" he answered.

"Your back. It's all scarred up!"

"That. That's where the master and the overseers

done beat me."

"Beat you? What…why…did they beat you?"

Even a child could pick up the weakness in my voice. I was floored. I didn't understand. Caleb turned around and sat on a bale of hay. I followed and did the same.

"When I don't do things the way they want me to, they take a stick or whip and hit me with it. They say, 'Caleb, you're not moving fast enough.' 'Caleb, get your head out of the clouds, boy.' 'Caleb, quit being lazy.' 'Caleb, can't you do anything right?' Even though I try my best, if it's not good enough or fast enough in their eyes, it don't matter."

He put his hands together like he was holding a stick himself. He raised them lingering above his head. WHAM! He brought them down with such force I shut my eyes on reflex. Even though it was imaginary in his hands, I could feel pain. It made me feel like that frog in Billy's hands–innocent yet butchered only because of its existence.

"Most times it's the overseers whooping me. Sometimes it's the master himself –whenever he feels like it." He closed his eyes; they started to water. Maybe inside his head he had seen something he didn't want to remember. "One time they said I was really bad. I don't remember what I done…I only remember them tying me to a tree. They swapped back and forth, each taking turns beating on me and laughing about it all the while."

He looked back up at me. His eyes were moist. My heart was heavy for him; my eyes started to water too. For some reason out of the blue, my mind thought back to yesterday when he told me, "I ain't never seen my daddy cry before–but I think after that offer from your pa he was gonna' burst."

I swore right then and there to myself I'd never forget what he said about his father, not even when I become a full-fledged man and lived to be a hundred. I promised myself to keep this burning alive in my memory all the days of my life. Seeing Caleb's back all chewed up like that had put a whole new meaning on his statement. If that kind of injustice could happen to a child, there was no way they'd hold it back from any man. What kind of monsters would do such a thing?

"Does the rest of your family have marks on them too?" I spoke timidly, half amazed, and half not meaning to offend. As I asked him, the scar on his uncle's face came to my mind.

Caleb nodded his head. "We all have them. We've all been marked by our masters, one after the other."

"How many masters you had, Caleb?"

"Only one so far as I remember. My daddy he ain't as strong as Rock, so he's been moved around quite a bit. He says more times than he has fingers to count. Till, probably by the grace of God, he comes to rest back at his mama's plantation again. My mama was bought up soon after. See that scar on her neck?" He pointed his finger under his jaw on the left side. I shook my head no.

"She got that from her last mistress before she was sold to our plantation. She was a house slave to her last mistress. Some things come up missing from her house, so she accused my mama of stealing. She held a knife to her throat, screaming, 'You tell me now! You better tell me where they're at or I'll slice you in half!'"

"Caleb!" Mr. Benjaman poked his head out from over the edge of the loft. "What do you think you doing, boy?"

"Nothing, just talking."

"Keep it down or we'll be caught for sure." He took a gander at me as his head disappeared. He looked as frustrated as my mother did about the floor. Maybe he was thinking that his son's shouting would bring the trackers. Or maybe he thought, why do we have to visit the past? I didn't know, it was hard to tell at times when you couldn't make sense of the world anymore.

"Anyway, that's how it was. Mama was sold off to my daddy's master. Later on she became pregnant with me. Next came Gloria. About the time Ivy come, our master bought Rock, which we later found out was Mama's brother."

"Is there anyone else in your family?"

"No, sir, none that I can think of. Grandma Thora had twelve kids and Pa is the only one that come back to her. She always said it was by the grace of God that that even happened. Mama and Rock found out that they have the same father but different mothers on account that their father was put out to stud by his master. I ain't seen no more of them. This here is the only family I got."

As I sat there and mulled over everything he told me, Pa came through the door. It startled Caleb; he jumped behind the bale we were sitting on. "It's alright," I whispered, "it's only my pa." Caleb stood back up.

"Jessie, let's go, Son. We got work to do." I got up and left. When I got next to Pa he asked quietly, "Why doesn't Caleb have a shirt on?"

"His shirt got torn but Ma is fixing it."

"Go get him one of yours in case his isn't done by tonight. Hurry up, Son, we got a lot of ground to cover."

I wondered what he meant by that statement, but I didn't give it too much thought. I ran in the house to my room. I picked out a nice shirt, thinking it would fit Caleb just fine. As I passed out the way of the kitchen, I noticed there were only two places set at the table. One was Nell's, the other was Ma's spot.

I went inside but Pa wasn't there. Caleb was in the same spot where we sat at before. I handed the shirt over to him. "Here, Caleb, see if this fits you."

His eyes got real big. "Wow! Thanks, Jessie!" He put it on and it was a little big on him but that was alright.

"You can borrow it until my ma is able to fix yours."

I believed he was so happy he didn't know what to do. So he hugged me. I didn't know how to take it, so I just let him. I never got a hug from another boy before, mostly from girls like Ma, Nell, and grandmothers when they came to visit. Sometimes I would get a hug from Pa–when I really needed it. One time though I did get a hug from Ike Josephson. It was the last time I was gonna' see him on account he was moving away and all. But I was a kid back then, so it was okay to cry when he finally left. You know what, I guess I had gotten a hug from a boy before. Knowing that made Caleb's hug seem not all bad.

He stepped back. "Thank you, Jessie, I'll never forget this."

I wanted to explain to him that I was only lending him the shirt, but it didn't seem all that important to mention. I walked out of the barn thinking perhaps it wasn't the shirt itself but maybe the fact that somebody would lend it to him that mattered.

Once outside I yelled for Pa. He answered me from back by the stable. I walked over and saw that Beatrice was hooked up to the wagon.

"What are you doing, Pa?" I asked, puzzled yet again.

"We, Son, are going for a ride. The best way north is up the Selah Valley. If we can get to the Mozzark River on the other side of the valley, they can follow that and be out of state territory two nights from now."

He climbed up in the driver's seat, I rode beside him. Between us was a basket of bread and two jugs of water. Pa whistled to Beatrice and we were off. I looked back at the house and barn like it was the last time I'd ever see them again.

"Mind you they won't be free yet, they'll just be out of the state. Once they're out of our state that thirty-five-dollar bounty on their lives is forfeited. They have to catch them on state territory in order to receive that money from the government."

"What if they catch them somewhere else and say they caught them in our state?"

"The trackers have to turn the family in to the proper authorities in order to go on record before they get paid. Then those authorities do an investigation around the local area to prove they captured the correct fugitives. If they lie, it should come out in the works of the investigation. That's the chance we have to take, but it's the only chance we have in our favor. We can't change the cards we're dealt, Jessie, only how we play our hand. After they get to the river, they're on their own the same as before they met us."

"It sounds to me like you don't wanna' turn them in. Is that right, Pa?"

"I did ask God for a sign. Maybe he's shown it to me, maybe he ain't. I can't really tell right now. So until I know for sure I'm gonna' listen to my conscience. If I don't follow my conscience, then why do I even have it in the first place? So no, I'm not gonna' turn the family in…not unless the Almighty himself says otherwise."

I was so happy right there I could've jumped out of my seat. That was the best news I'd heard all day, probably the best news I'd heard since Caleb's family had been here–even better than Ma being pregnant (no offense to her, of course). Ma knew it, and now I knew it for sure…Pa was a honest man, and in time he'd always do what was right.

We had to pass through town on the way to Selah Valley. It was so robust and alive, a real gem of a community. Maybe it was the mood I was in, but the people appeared to be happier than usual. Everyone walked up and down the street appearing not to have a care in the world. Most of the people we knew smiled and waved to us as we went by. Naturally Pa and I waved back. It was a pure delight to be living next to such fine, outstanding folks.

The way Pa had it planned it would take us four hours to reach the bend in the Mozzark River, four hours one way through the valley until they could follow it north. We trotted a slow pace as to keep Beatrice's strength up for the whole journey. Pa explained that we were taking this route today to make sure everything would go off without a hitch.

We stopped where Pa believed the river to bend. Beatrice got herself a quick rest and a meal of bagged oats. The two of us munched on loaves of bread for our dinner. Pa said Ma was feeding Mr. Benjaman and the family tonight. That was good; I was starting to worry about them not being taken care of while we were gone. Tomorrow night Ma was planning on cooking beef stew for them before they left.

It was very pretty out there, all lush, green, and wild. A person could live out there forever. It was so peaceful you felt as though the very hand of God was in this place. If heaven were ever close to Earth, it would've been right there, I reckon. Pa and I could've very well been standing in the garden of Eden.

When we started our way back, the sun began to get low to the right of us. Pa figured we'd hit town a hour or so after sundown. That was good, not as good as eating dinner in paradise, but good just the same. I was so happy I felt like dancing. After all the twists, turns, and bumps in my way, today nothing could've gotten any better.

Night had set in just like Pa said, but when we started reaching town we saw a strange, orange glow of light ahead of us. To the south edge of town we saw a fire. Pa, thinking that perhaps one of the buildings was on fire, hurried Beatrice along to see if they needed any help. As our wagon galloped down Main Street, everyone was either standing still or looking away in horror. "Why doesn't anyone help?" I wondered.

The fire, it turned out, was not one of the buildings, but rather in the middle of the road. It was a bonfire almost as tall as a two-story building. There were some figures on horseback riding around it. I could hear pistols firing before my eyes could adjust to the change in this darkness. Three horses danced around the bonfire, and one figure with his back turned to the town was watching everything take place.

"Night riders," Pa gasped.

I took another good look and saw all three horsemen were dressed in white sheets like ghosts. It was easy to tell they were men under their hoods because of the way they whooped and hollered. One of the men was riding around holding up a scarecrow. The person on the ground just stood there. He wasn't dressed in white, but wore normal attire I'd say for any average man about town. He wasn't doing anything to stop this insanity. He just watched it take place…like giving some kind of silent approval.

We got close enough to the fire now but were still in the town's borders. Pa stopped Beatrice. She was scared, and whinnied up in the air. This caused the figure to turn around and peer straight at us.

It was Tom Navin.

"Evening, Jonathan," he said with the bonfire behind him. It looked like the very backdrop of hell itself. "What brings you out here tonight?"

The horsemen stopped to gather around our cart on all sides. I was scared so I got real close to Pa and clutched his arm. Frantically I looked around, seeing all kinds of thing in the background, women holding their hands over their mouths as they ran away while their men were leading them to safety. I saw that the scarecrow the rider was carrying had a black face and hair just like a colored person. I could see more scarecrows just like that one hanging in trees from nooses. I looked at one of the horses breathing hard next to us, and even though its head was under a sheet, I swore it was an Appaloosa. That made me believe that these three night riders were the very same trackers I met earlier today. I never had the notion to tell Pa about them, but now it was too late.

"Well, Jonathan, what brings you out here at this time of night?" As Mr. Navin spoke, the sound of hissing and crackling from the fire hung in the air. The horses neighed at all corners of us and stood uneasy, like cats ready to pounce. Beatrice wanted to bolt, but Tom Navin was blocking her. It was so stressful I could've jumped out of my skin in a heartbeat.

"We went up to check on ol' Doug Richman," Pa said to Navin. "Heard he was sick. Turns out he was just lonely."

"We need to check your wagon!" boomed the rider on the Appaloosa. "Do we have your permission?"

Pa turned, staring at him. "No, you do not."

"We're just gonna' check it anyway," said one in a gruff voice. "It would just be easier for ya'll if we did."

"Hold on, fellas," Billy's dad demanded, holding his arm up to them. "Now, Jonathan, you're making yourself look mighty unfriendly here. All we wanna' do is check your wagon for stowaways."

"Tom," Pa replied, "if you want to check my wagon, then go ahead. But I don't let no strangers go through my business."

Tom Navin took his cane and poked it into our covered cart. He walked all around, even jumping in the back to look under our burlap coverings. Finally he jumped out and came to the front again. "See, boys, nothing to worry about. Not even a trace of Negroes have been in there. He's all clear."

"Why are you doing this? Having this display and all." I could see Pa's fist was clenched on the reins. At first I thought he was scared, but now I'd say he was more mad than anything else.

"Heard those Negroes were around these parts," one of the riders shouted. "We're just trying to discourage those who would take a notion to help them! And to smoke them out in the process."

"Assisting runaway slaves is a felony in these parts," declared another one. "It would be best if you tell us what you know about the situation."

"Wouldn't want any friends of Mr. Navin here to get caught up in the crossfire," the gruff rider replied, then rode up next to the fire and threw the scarecrow in.

"Yes, Jonathan," Mr. Navin added, "If you know anything, do tell. I'll make sure you get a reward and no trouble will come to you and your family afterwards. Unless, of course, you had known something before and not revealed it earlier. You have my solemn promise, if you do know anything about their whereabouts, you can come clean right now and nothing will ever happen to you and your kin over it."

I was so scared I wanted to tell them where they were right then and there. I felt all my nerves going and sweat pouring out of every inch of my body. I clutched Pa's shirt so hard I thought it would rip. The only thing that kept me from talking was watching that scarecrow burn. It made me think of Caleb's back. It made me remember him saying how his daddy was traded more times than he had fingers to count. It made me remember his uncle's scar and how he couldn't talk right 'cause of what happened to him. It made me imagine some lady holding a knife to his mama's throat, screaming. 'You tell me now! You better tell me where they're at or I'll slice you in half.' Almost gonna' die before she even met his daddy, before she could give birth to him.

It made me think back as to why they were so scared at first. Scared at being in the daylight. Scared enough to jump out of their skins the first time they saw me. Scared enough not to take roads. But to wander around in the dark, in the woods, not really having any idea where it would take them. Scared enough to have a pregnant woman break down and cry not knowing what they were gonna' do to her unborn baby if they were caught.

These men weren't fixing to burn pillows... but burn people.

"Please, Pa, please do what's right," I thought. Only God could protect them from this type of evil, but right now their very lives were hanging on the next words that would come out of his mouth. I was scared, I wanted to go home, but I'd been living in paradise already compared to Caleb's family. "Do the right thing, Pa, in God's name, please do the right thing."

"No, sir, I can't say that I do know anything."

"Very well, Jonathan, I can trust your honesty," Navin stated, stepping out of the way toward my side of the wagon. Then he looked at me curiously. "Something wrong, Jessie?"

With all this going on, I kind of hoped they forgot I was even there. I didn't know if the three horsemen knew it, but Billy's dad knew I was terrified. He began to stare more intently at me.

"All this excitement is spooking him," Pa said, putting his hand on my knee. "I need to get him home."

"It's the way of the world, Jonathan," Tom Navin stated, turning his attention back toward Pa. "You can't keep him a child forever. If we're gonna' stay on top, then we have to make sure everyone else, including those Negroes, stays in their place."

With that, Pa whistled to Beatrice and we were finally off. The three riders with Tom Navin stood there watching us go. Maybe they were talking to each other. Maybe they were gloating, confident in the message they delivered. I didn't care–I just wanted to go. Curving around the fire, their suits disappeared into the lap of flames.

As we finished making our turn around the bonfire, I saw Billy on the other side. He was so fixated on the inferno he didn't even notice our cart go by. There he was, like a statue, hypnotized by the flames. His eyes were as wide as they could be, his mouth opened in awe, but not a drop of sweat on his face near as I could tell. We turned 'round the bend in the road leading out of town and he was still standing there…a silhouette in an all consuming backdrop of flames.

Chapter 8: When we get home...

When we got home, both Pa and I could barely drag our feet in. The last leg from town felt longer than the entire trip put together. After we had finally gotten away from that sight, I told Pa to stop or I was gonna' soil my overalls. Once we were going again, neither one of us could dare say another word. Shocked, mortified, dumbfounded–those words paled in comparison to the emptiness I was feeling, like my soul had been ripped out, leaving me as hollow as an empty well.

Nell was asleep when we reached the house. I was the first one in; Pa unhitched Beatrice and led her back to the stable. Ma sat in our back room stitching Caleb's shirt. She looked up at me and immediately knew something was wrong. She rushed over and knelt down in front of me. She clasped her hands at the sides of my face, making me look eye-to-eye with her.

"What's wrong? Are you alright? Your face is as white as a ghost–what happened?"

I tried not to cry but I wasn't very good at it. I burst out sobbing like a newborn baby. All Ma could do was hug me next to her and rock us back and forth, comforting me like only a mother knew best. I was so weak I trembled in her arms until I collapsed on the floor.

The door opened, and Pa walked in. There was no color in his face either. Ma stood up and opened her arms. They received each other while I was squeezed onto Ma's leg, crying. All of this distressed Ma too, so she joined in. Sometimes there just ain't any words to express a sorrowful feeling.

After a time I was able to stop. I sniffled my way up from the floor. I didn't know if Pa had whispered anything to Ma, but she tried to compose herself while I looked at them.

"Jessie," Pa squeaked out, "we've had a hard day. Go to your room, and try to get some sleep."

It was a lonely walk up those stairs to my room. I lay in my bed too distressed to even take my clothes off. I could hear both my parents muttering downstairs. Then I heard Ma and Pa both crying together again. I did my best to close my eyes and fall asleep though it was hard. Right now I couldn't tell whether they were crying over the horror we had just seen tonight, or over what Caleb's family might expect to go through if they got caught.

Morning came too soon, again. I knew I had slept but I didn't feel rested, yet again. I unwillingly trudged my way downstairs to start the day. No one was in the kitchen, so I just stood there a minute by myself. Nell whizzed past me from the back room, making her rag doll fly like a bird.

"Are you up, Jessie?" Ma called from the back room. My parents were both there. Ma was peeling potatoes; Pa was reading his Bible. "I'm glad to see you're finally up. It's almost noon."

Noon, where had the day gone already? Nell ran by again. No one seemed to notice. My parents seemed calm and collected compared to the night before.

"Are you excited? Today's the big day!" Ma said real cheerful-like.

"Big day? What big day?"

"The day, silly, when you and Pa are gonna' help send the family off at the state line. I was gonna' suggest that you take a nap this afternoon so you'll be plenty rested for your journey. But you got up so late I guess you won't need to."

"I'll take mine later, thanks," Pa stated without looking up from his table. "You don't need to take one unless you wanna."

"Am I dreaming or have they gone crazy?" I asked myself, then I blurted out, "What about last night? Aren't you scared?"

Pa turned around to face the two of us. He placed his elbows on his knees and clasped his hands together under his chin. Perhaps he was thinking of what I just said, or reflecting on what he had decided to do. Maybe he was thinking of the best way to tell me his decision, or of how to avoid my question. Finally he motioned for me to come over to him.

"Son, remember when you found me asking God for a sign?"

"Yes, sir," I said, wondering where he was going.

"Well, he did. God showed us a sign last night that what we are doing is right. Now it's not the kind of thing the two of us wanted to see, but that's the future that lies in store for Mr. Benjaman and his family if we don't act. If we had just sat on our hands and done nothing the first night they came, they might be facing that horrible fate as we speak.

"We gave them a chance to rest. All we can do now is release them and pray for their safety. They are, and will always be, in God's hands."

"You mean God did want us to help the family be free?"

"I don't believe the Almighty would've let them endure all they've been through to get up here just so they could get caught."

"You also have to think about the Golden Rule, Jessie," Ma chimed in, "to treat other people the way you'd like to be treated. If you were on the road hungry and half dead, wouldn't you want someone to help you?" I nodded my head yes. "We should always help those in need when it's in our ability to act."

"What about all those lies we've been telling?" I inquired.

"Son, you have to think of the greater good. There

are people's lives at stake. What do you think matters more to the Lord, worrying about what other people think, or helping someone in need?"

I started to perk right up. We were living out scripture and I didn't even know it, just like we were helping that man on the road in that story of the good Samaritan. It made me feel pretty good inside, knowing it was in God's best interest for Caleb's family to be free.

"Yes, Son," Pa continued, "to do good by other folks, even if they don't have the ability to pay you back, is a blessing to both parties. Even if nobody else in the world knows–the Lord knows. And it pleases him to see his children doing right by others. When you do it with a pure heart, not looking for anything in return, it's a beautiful thing in itself. Kind of like when the butterflies come in autumn."

Both Ma and I were taken aback. I guess we never expected Pa to think on such things.

Before we knew it, there was a knock on the front door. I ran to see who it was. It was Billy Navin.

"Jessie," he said excitedly, "there was a bonfire in town last night. You wanna' go see what's left of it?"

I hesitated to speak. It was clear he didn't know about our encounter with his father last night. I didn't wanna' go because I didn't want to be reminded of it. Not only that, but I thought it would be best if I kept plenty of distance between myself and the Navins. On account of last night's fire (and Billy's drastic frog-killing personality), who knew what else could possibly come to the surface.

"I'll have to check with Pa." With that, I left him waiting at the screen door. Going back to my parents in the back room, I told them, "It's Billy Navin. He wants me to go with him to town–but I don't wanna' go."

"Does he know we were up there last night?"

"No, I don't believe so."

Pa thought hard for a minute, enough to where he leaned back and pinched his fingers over his eyes. When he swung forward, he told me, "Go with him."

"What!" Ma exclaimed.

"But," I declared.

"Go with him, just for today. Two hours should be enough to satisfy him."

"But," I interrupted, not knowing if he heard me the first time.

"It's just until we get the family out of here. I don't need no son of Navin snooping around or suspecting nothing till we get our job done. We've come this close already; we can't let the family down. Tomorrow you have my permission to beat him to a pulp if you need to, but today is the day that matters."

Reluctantly I walked to town with Billy. I listened to him go on and on while making it sound like I was interested. If his father didn't tell him I was there, why should I? When we finally made it to the edge of town, there were a whole lot of people cleaning up the burnt rubble from the night before. Thankfully the scarecrows were already down and taken away. The rest of the burnt mess was in the process of being hauled away on carts. I figured there were about twelve to fifteen men in the whole process, from loading carts down to scrubbing the dirt road so there was not a trace of what happened. That's just the way it goes I guess–evil men set fires and innocent men have to clean up the mess left behind.

Billy was disappointed that there wasn't much damage to see. So we ended up walking around mostly. As we did, a lot of the town's folk spied crossly at the two of us. Some of them whispered to each other as we went by. I hoped they were talking about Billy's family and not mine. Billy didn't seem to notice as the two of us meandered on. Besides, Billy was doing all the talking between us, mostly about nothing, so it was no wonder why he didn't notice. I myself stayed pretty quiet with my head held low. One time he did ask me if I was alright. I told him I was a little sick. Then I gave a cough. I don't know how he bought it, but it worked for the meantime anyway.

All of a sudden we saw the trackers. Two of them were on top of their horses, and one walked his on the ground. They all came up Main Street. All three men looked mighty angry. Some men pulled their women closer to the buildings, out of their way. Everyone did their best to avoid them. They looked as though they could bite your head off the first chance they got. Maybe they were so angry 'cause the hate spilled out of them and they couldn't hold it back no more. Maybe it was because their little stunt didn't work like they had planned. Nobody was jumping forward handing any coloreds to them. Maybe their luck had run out here and they knew they had to leave empty-handed. Whatever it was, they were looking like wounded animals ready to snap.

One of the riders locked eyes on Billy and me. The one on the ground was shouting at some people huddled by a store. "Where are those Negroes at! Somebody's gotta' be hiding them!" I was so mesmerized by his scare tactic, I neglected to see the other two ride up until they were on top of us.

"Hello, boys," the gruff one snorted.

It startled me. I stumbled back against a horse's end.

"Where do you think you're going?" he barked.

"Billy," the leader said, "we're run out of time and out of patience."

"If your father isn't able to give us any proper leads," the gruff one continued, "we're just gonna have to improvise."

"All his daddy's leads have led to nothing!" The third one joined in. He broke between the other two and grabbed my shirt with his fist. We were nose-to-nose. "You know where that Negro family is, don't you, boy."

He breathed hot on me. I tried to squirm away, but he just got closer. "Tell me where they are or you'll live to regret it!"

Billy shouted, "Leave him alone, he don't know nothing!" The man pushed him away. Billy fell under a horse and rolled out, leaving me alone in the circle of bandits.

"WHERE ARE THEY? TELL ME WHERE ARE THOSE SLAVES! WHERE'S THAT NEGRO FAMILY HIDING AT?"

"Slave family? I've seen a slave family!" Someone called out, all three men looked toward his direction. The angry one let go of me to saddle his horse. Without another word, all three men headed toward the individual. I couldn't see who it was, so I scurried off to the side. It was Luke. He stood on the other side of the street while the three horsemen came up to him.

Once I scrambled to my feet, Billy pulled me out of the way. Trying to drag me into a building, I did my best to keep him off so I could yell. "Luke, don't tell them anything!" But all that was able to come out of me was "Luke!"

The three men snapped their heads back my way. The one closest in my direction placed his hand on the revolver to his side where I could see. Then he cocked it. When Billy saw that, he let go of me and ran into the building. I stopped immediately from saying the rest and froze as silent as a statue. After that they all turned their attention back to Luke. There I was less than a hundred yards away…and powerless to do anything.

"Come again?" the one with the Appaloosa asked.

"I said I saw a slave family," Luke repeated.

The two sidekicks looked at each other, but the leader didn't seem convinced. "Boy, we've run into nothing but dead ends since we hit this town. We're not playing around here. Now tell me, how many of them did you see so it'll help us believe you."

"Seven," Luke said confidently. "Two of them are little girls; one's a pregnant mother."

The two henchmen nodded to each other; still the leader asked, "What do the other four look like?"

"What does it matter what they look like, they look like coloreds. But if it doesn't match the description of who you're looking for, then maybe it's the wrong family."

Luke turned to step away. The head man slapped his hand on Luke's shoulder and spun him back toward them. "It does match. Now tell me, where did you see them!"

Luke gazed at the man indignantly. Then he took his hand to grab the tracker's. While he swung it off him, he asked, "Why, what's in it for me?"

"Excuse me…uhm Luke…is it?" The head man was speaking more gingerly now. Perhaps he was waking up to the fact his last chance could be walking away. "You see, son, helping escaped convicts and runaway slaves is a federal crime. It can land you in some serious trouble. Now you've already conveyed to us that you know about the whereabouts and existence of this Negro family we're searching for. It would be in your best interest to tell us where they are so that no form of penalty comes back on you."

"He means jail," the second one piped in.

"That's right," the leader continued. "If you have had any foreknowledge of this escaped family, and you fail to release it, you will go to jail."

He allowed Luke a minute to step back and ponder this notion. The two in the background nodded confidently at each other, almost like saying either, "Now we got them," or "Now we got him."

"Now, Luke, the truth is you only have two options, my friend. One is to keep what you know, get locked up, and sit there wondering if it did them any good 'cause they're just gonna' get caught anyway. Or…tell us what you know and save yourself from a heap of trouble. And as a reward for your help in their capture, we'll guarantee you seventy-five cents per head on all seven of them once we have them. Now, Luke, you look like a smart young man–which do you think you should choose? Now, where did you say you saw them at?"

The suspense was so thick you could cut it with a knife. I was praying inside myself that Luke didn't say anything. But if Luke kept silent they said he'd go to jail. If he did speak up, then Caleb's family and mine would suffer. I hoped God was listening 'cause I didn't see this going well at all.

"Shiloh, I saw them when I was in Shiloh."

The three stared at each other. The gruff one whispered "Shiloh," only he sounded more concerned than relieved.

"Shiloh," the leader stated questionably. "You say you saw them in Shiloh? That's a six hour ride from here."

"Yep, that's where I saw them at. I was in Shiloh all yesterday and just got back this morning, ask anybody. While I was there I saw them along the river down there bathing and such. I think if they follow it down to the valley, they might be able to find a shallow place to forge across."

"How in the world did they end up going that far west?" the second one commented to his companions.

"You can't expect Negroes to know their way in the dark," the gruff one retorted.

"Listen, boy," the head man replied. "We're professional trackers. All their signs lead to here and none of them lead out. You expect us to believe that that family was able to make it that far west and still be over a day ahead of us?"

"Call me a liar if you want to. But if you don't get moving, somebody else is gonna' catch your bounty."

With that Luke walked away, leaving the three talking to each other. I heard one of them say, "What choice do we have? There's nothing left for us here." Then the three trackers took off as fast as their horses could carry them, out of town–toward Shiloh.

I stood there in wonder of the whole experience. Did I just see Luke, a jittery old farmhand, take on three barbarian bounty hunters and come out on top? Wasn't he the same man who threatened to turn my family in if I spoke up? What was going on here?

As Luke crossed the street over to my side, Billy slunk his way next to me again. He was not his usual boastful self; in fact, Billy's head hung low, like he was ashamed. I guess being scared like that put a little bit of humility in him for the time being, I reckon.

"Morning, fellas," Luke said. "Oh, Jessie, I've got something for you."

He reached in his pocket. I was still in awe, so he grabbed my hand and plopped his closed fist in it. When he pulled back, I saw my hand was full of coins, mostly pennies.

"Whoa, you're rich," Billy declared, standing next to me.

"He's not rich, I borrowed it from him. I did have to use eleven cents out of it though. A man's gotta' eat on his travels."

Next thing I knew Luke leaned down to my ear so Billy couldn't hear him. He whispered…"I hope you understand I was just playing with you the other day. Your family has always been so kind putting up with me. I wouldn't want to lose face with your ma and pa after they've always been so kind to me all these years. They really have made me feel like part of your family."

When he stood up, he rubbed my head and declared, "I'll see you tomorrow, Jessie. Good afternoon, gentlemen." With that he walked off, whistling to himself. As I put the money into my pocket, I smiled. You know what, I do believe I liked it when he rubbed my head like that.

I was in no mood to stay in town after that, so I ran home, leaving Billy behind. I was all anxious to tell my ma and pa everything that happened. I ran inside the house and called for my parents, but no one answered. I thundered through the rooms downstairs, then worked my way up. I almost bolted into Nell's room, but I saw her lying on her bed so I backed out easy. I headed into my parents' bedroom.

Pa was laying down, and before I could say anything, he muttered, "Be quiet, I'm trying to sleep." Creeping out of there, I checked the rest of the rooms for my ma quietly, but she was nowhere to be seen. I decided to head outside past the kitchen where the stew was simmering and go toward the barn.

In the barn I heard the sound of talking, so I looked in before I entered. Sitting on chairs were my ma, Miz Sarah, and the old lady, just talking with each other without a care in the world, like most women do anyways. My ma was working on Caleb's shirt while Miz Sarah was feeding her thread.

As I entered the door creaked. The three women immediately stopped and looked at me. I guess they must've realized there was no threat, because without warning they were right back talking again exactly where they left off. I went up to Ma instinctively even though I didn't really know how to begin to tell her about my experience. Where should I begin–Luke making me believe he was gonna' turn us in, the trackers, or Luke tricking them all out of town. So many choices–I wished they'd be quiet for a minute so I could think.

"Hi, sweetie," Ma said, kissing me on the forehead. "It's good that you're home so soon."

"This young man has been a blessing," the old lady stated. "Real helpful, honest, and true."

"Uhm-hum," Miz Sarah added, "it's true. And Caleb just looovvvves you. You're probably the best friend he's ever had. He ain't ever had any one else close to his age to play with except his sisters."

I looked around. I saw the girls chasing each other on the floor, but I didn't see Caleb. "Where is he?" I asked.

"The men are up there sleeping," Miz Sarah pointed out, "to be ready for tonight. They let us sleep in earlier; now it's their turn. We had to take shifts watching, being on the road and all."

"Yes, and thank God you've been able to rest," my ma chimed in. "We wouldn't want that baby to come too early now." All three women nodded their heads together. "What are you gonna' to call it?"

"Well," Miz Sarah went on to say, "Benjaman and I haven't had much time to think. What ya'll gonna' call yours?"

"Well, Jonathan had given our younger daughter Nell the responsibility of coming up with a name. Actually I think it's more or less a way to keep her out of trouble, she's not even four after all. Anyway the only words she can come up with are vegetables, things around the house, and ones she's made up herself, stuff like that. Well, in the middle of all this nonsense she comes up with the name Immanuel. I'm surprised, so I ask her, 'Where did you come up with that name, honey?' She just shrugs her shoulders and says, 'I don't know, it just came to me.'"

"Immanuel," the old lady sat back and pondered. "I think I heard that name before."

"What does it mean, Mama?" Miz Sarah asked her mother-in-law.

"It means 'God with us,'" my ma proclaimed.

"Immanuel," Miz Sarah reflected. "Immanuel. I wonder if that can be a boy's name or a girl's name."

"It don't matter either way. It sounds just fine," the old lady declared.

"I think I'll tell my husband I want the baby to be called Immanuel then. After all we've been through, it seems only fitting." The three women nodded their heads again.

Just then the door creaked open. The women stopped yacking (just like before when I came in). To everyone's surprise little Nell stepped into the barn. Rubbing the sleep from her eyes, she said, "Ma, there you are."

She waddled over to Ma and started to climb on her lap. Ma handed Miz Sarah Caleb's shirt and things.

Nell laid her head on our mother's chest. Ma kissed her on her head, then told her, "You're suppose to be asleep, little one."

Oops, I guess that was my fault. I didn't mean to wake anybody when I came charging through the house like I did.

"Ohh how precious," Miz Sarah remarked.

Nell rolled her head over in Miz Sarah's direction, and her eyes opened up wide. Nell had NEVER seen colored people before. I wondered how she was going to react. She lifted her head up toward Miz Sarah, still astonished.

"Hi there, cutie," the old lady said, giving Nell a little wave.

Nell turned her attention toward her now. She slid off Ma's lap and went over to her. This made the old lady chuckle on the inside. Nell looked at her hand and took hold of it. She studied it on every side from every angle. Finally the little girl gazed up at the lady and asked…"Why ya'll different?"

Ma didn't know what to say. Miz Sarah was speechless, the same as I. But for some reason this made the old lady laugh.

"Sweet child," she said while placing her hand on the side of Nell's head. "Because God is an artist. Ever see the sunrise or the sunset? Ever seen the leaves change colors in the fall? God is an artist. The world is his canvas; so are you and me. He makes everyone just a little bit different. Some folks is boys, some folks is girls. But even that don't stop him from making folks the same, and a little bit special from the rest. Look at your ma and Miz Sarah. They're both girls just the same, but still a little bit different from each other. Now look at Miz Sarah and me. We're both the same, and different from each other too."

"God made all of you," Nell replied.

"Uhm-hum. And he made the sky, the trees, the water, the mountains, everything.

And he never stops running out of ideas."

"Wooowww!" Nell stated in childlike wonder.

She turned to me, saying, "Remember this, Jessie, and remember it good, you hear? The Lord says that everything he does is right… and he is the one who made them both. Selah–stop and think–that's all you need to know for now."

Gloria and Ivy came over. "You wanna' come play?" Nell nodded her head yes.

They grabbed her by the hands and led her into the patch of sunlight left by the roof door. All the women, and myself included, sat there in amazement and quiet contentment as the children sang, "Ring around the rosies. Pocket full of posies. Ashes, ashes, we all fall down."

The girls got up and did it over and over again. It kind of made me smile on the inside. It was a funny kind of joy–you can't explain it. Seeing those girls dance made me feel like the butterflies had come already.

That night after dark Pa hitched up Beatrice to the wagon. I could see him faintly outside throwing in extra burlap sacks. We didn't plan to get caught, but the sacks were there to hide the family in case we did run into somebody. Next he put in a pack of food for the family. Then he drove the wagon close to the barn. One by one the family slipped out and into the bed of our wagon.

Ma was standing next to me as we looked out the back room window. The two of us watched as each person disappeared under the coverings. It was a heart wrenching moment in my life, but I knew full well it had to be done. The only thing that got me though the agony of saying goodbye was the hope that our Maker was watching out for them. Ma sighed, then said, "Go on, Jessie." But before I could walk away, she placed both her hands on my head so I would look up at her. She was a bit teary eyed when she brought her face close up to mine.

"I...am...proud...of...you."

She kissed me on the forehead, gave me a hug, then sent me off. I put on a jacket while walking to the cart, then climbed in the front bench and waited. I felt the last of Caleb's family crawl around under the sacks. Pa climbed up in the bench along with me. He took the reins, then looked at me. I could almost feel him say, "We've been in this together this far, now it's time to finish it together." Next thing I knew, he whistled to Beatrice and we were off.

Going through town was mighty quiet. Only a few lights in the windows. No people on the street. Just the way you'd like it for a mission like this. It was very relieving to head out of town without a hitch.

Four hours dragged themselves by. Pa and I made small talk to keep ourselves awake (not near as bad as the women in the barn though). It seemed almost as long as the ride home from town last night. Pa said to Mr. Benjaman he'd give a word if there was any trouble, so they could try to sleep. Only Caleb and the little ones were able to though; the rest stayed quiet and alert. I think it was due to the anticipation of what lay ahead.

Before we made it to the river my ma's voice echoed back in my head: "I am proud of you." I was glad she said it even though I didn't really know why. I was only trying to treat folks the way I would've wanted them to treat me. That was all, nothing really spectacular about that. In fact, it just came easy with a little practice.

The sound of the river was flowing through the night air. Normally a river sounds pretty powerful, but for some reason or another this one sounded kind of sad. Maybe it knew we'd come here to say goodbye.

The wagon stopped. The adults sat up and stretched themselves. Miz Sarah woke up the girls, and Mr. Benjaman woke up Caleb. Rock helped the old lady down out of the wagon first; Miz Sarah and the girls followed. Last came Caleb and Mr. Benjaman. Those two stood close to us while the others were in a line behind them.

"Goodbye, Jessie. I'll never forget you." Caleb hugged me and I hugged him back. He stepped back to line up with the rest of his family. I wanted to tell him to write, but I knew he couldn't. Just a note in the mail saying "We Made It" would be good–but even if he could, that might jeopardize his family for months to come. It was best to keep him locked in my memory. Even though I would miss him, he would be free. And what was freedom worth? To him it meant leaving everything he had known in hopes of a better life, one without masters and overseers, beatings, and threats to his family's lives. He would always have a place in my heart along with the Lord. He would always live in my memory. He would always be free to me.

Mr. Benjaman and Pa shook hands; when they finished they didn't let go. They both looked at each other a little while. It seemed the two had formed a bond and neither one of them wanted to say goodbye. I knew how they felt.

"I wish I could take you farther," Pa said regretfully, "but I gotta' boy coming tomorrow morning. He might get suspicious if I'm not there."

"It's alright. You've already done enough for us as it is."

"But how will you find your way?"

"Last night I asked the Lord, 'Which way should we go?' He said to me, 'Follow the Drinking Gourd.'"

Mr. Benjaman looked up at the night sky. This caused everyone else to do the same. And wouldn't you know it, right there in the middle of all of God's creation was a soup ladle made out of stars. It was shining brighter than all the other ones, yet I don't recall ever seeing it before. I wondered, had it always been up there like that, or did the Lord make it special for just such an occasion?

The two men looked back at each other. Then Pa said, "I asked the Lord one night to show me a sign too. While I was praying, I knocked over my Bible. When I picked it up, it was turned to Matthew 25. When I read it, it said that' "the King will say to those on his right, 'Come, you who are blessed by my Father; take your inheritance, the kingdom prepared for you since the creation of the world. For I was hungry and you gave me something to eat, I was thirsty and you gave me something to drink, I was a stranger and you invited me in, I needed clothes and you clothed me, I was sick and you looked after me, I was in prison and you came to visit me.'

"'Then the righteous will answer him, 'Lord, when did we see you hungry and feed you, or thirsty and give you something to drink? When did we see you a stranger and invite you in, or needing clothes and clothe you? When did we see you sick or in prison and go to visit you?'

"'The King will reply, 'I tell you the truth, whatever you did for one of the least of these brothers of mine, you did for me.'"

"When we get home," Mr. Benjaman said, "we're

gonna' remember ya'll. And we're gonna' tell our Daddy all about the things you done for us in this world. Even though I believe he knows it already."

The two men hugged each other…then it was goodbye. Mr. Benjaman led his family down the river in a thicket of brush. The woods engulfed them. We climbed aboard our wagon and listened to their movements until the sound of the river drowned them out.

Pa gave a hoot like an owl. One of Caleb's family hooted back to us. He waited another minute or so and Pa did it again. This time it was more faded than before. Another minute, then he did it again. This time there was no response.

Well…it was done.

Pa turned the wagon around and we started making the long trek home, there in the dark alone, and lonely. I tried not to cry but I wasn't very good at it. Pa threw his arm over my shoulder and hugged me close. I couldn't stop, I didn't even let myself try. Did you ever do a work and then cry at the end of the process when you had to leave it? 'Cause you knew deep down in your heart that it changed you and you'd never be the same. I did.

I cried so much on the way home that I must've cried myself to sleep, like Nell did sometimes when she wouldn't take a nap. I had a dream that Caleb and I were running wild and free in a field full of sunlight. We were both laughing and carrying on without a care in the world.

All of a sudden the butterflies came. They were all around us, so thick we could hardly see each other. There the two of us stood in awe and wonder. Then without warning, I felt myself being lifted up, Caleb too. Both of us went higher and higher into the air along with the butterflies.

They carried us over the field, then the woods. We flew over town and all the people looked like ants. Higher we went, both he and I together, until we came to a mountain and passed around it. We were so high even the clouds were below us. I saw a thundercloud from below flashing lightning all in itself. Such wonders I had never imagined before in my whole life. It was so amazing neither one of us could speak. Then gentle as could be, we floated down on top of a cloud.

It must of been a reflex that my eyes opened up, because I for one never wanted to leave that dream. I saw the ceiling to my room and a figure standing over me. The last thing I could remember seeing before I closed my eyes again was my father's face, clear in the moonlight, dropping me off in my bed.

It sure did feel like I was flying…only it turned out that I was being lifted in my father's arms.

Epilogue

We never got caught. It sure is a blessing to know God is on your side when you do the right thing. I guess when you do the right thing, he allows things just to follow you wherever you go.

Billy Navin and I did officially end our friendship several years later. I thought I could be a positive influence on him, but it turned out that I couldn't. It happened one day when we got into a fistfight over a girl that neither one of us ended up marrying anyway. We knocked ourselves halfway across town until both of us decided we had had enough.

He yelled back at me with his nose covered in blood, "I HATE YA'! I DON'T EVER WANNA' SEE YA' NO MORE!" For the longest time I thought he was gonna' ambush me and stick me with that knife of his. It never happened. Just goes to show you that a coward is a coward whether he wears a sheet or not.

The last I heard about Tom Navin was he took an

illness real bad the last couple years of his life. The last week he was alive he spent in bed, coughin' up blood until he finally choked on it. After his dad died, Billy moved farther south and I never heard another word about him again.

It would turn out Luke would be a greater help to my family over the years than any of us could ever imagine back when we started our first mission. The man always loved to travel, but his heart stayed close to our home. He would stop by a couple times a year to visit. He went everywhere, north to south, and told us stories from all over. He also told us of other "safe houses" for runaways to hide in and how to get them there. We would later take that information and use it to direct more of God's children seekin' freedom. A few years before he died, he said the slaves had a name for what we did, starting that summer and ever since then. They called it the Underground Railroad.

My sister Nell grew up and married. She moved up North to Pennsylvania with her husband. The two of them spend their lives up there helping out runaways, supplying them with food and relocating them to safe places. She always tells me that of all her earliest memories of childhood, the one where she spoke to Caleb's grandmother comes up the most. I guess their appearance in our humble hay barn changed her too, when she wasn't looking. I guess it just runs in the family.

Every night after Caleb's family left, Pa would go

outside and play his harmonica, no matter the weather; hot or cold, dry or wet, except of course when it snowed. He knew no slave would run away in the winter due to the cold and the tracks in the snow. Sometimes we would get extra company coming in under the moonlight. Luke also suggested that we hang a quilt over our porch railing as a signal.

My parents are gone now to be with the Lord. All my brothers and sisters have moved on to other places, leaving just me and my family at the old farmhouse. When my father died he left each of us an inheritance. Some of it was more than anybody could ever put a dollar amount on, namely, a good name and character to live by. That's the funny thing about those two traits: even though it might hurt sometimes to develop them, you're always glad you have them in the end.

To me he left the house, the farm, and the harmonica. I still play it every night, that is, whenever I can wrestle it away from my grandchildren. I play it partly for him, partly for others who are traveling, mostly for the Lord. Pa and I never figured we would be part of something that would mean anything. We were just doing our best to treat other people with the type of dignity God said they deserve.

I don't know why my father showed so much kindness to our first family, other than him living by the Golden Rule. Maybe he took to them because Miz Sarah and my mother were both pregnant at the same time. Maybe he had sympathy that girls about my sister's age could be auctioned off like pieces of meat. Maybe it was those things and a bit more–who knows. It's just one of those events in life where you don't need to know why. You just thank God you were there for it, to take part in making a difference in someone else's life when it mattered most to them.

I don't get out to see the butterflies like I used too. I've seen them enough in my day. Plus now I get the joy of my grandchildren's experiences with them. I have another way all my own to experience that same joy that it brings, if you know what I mean.

I don't know how many people the Lord has allowed my family to help over the years, perhaps fifty, maybe more, only he knows. Some of them I've even led to the Lord myself. Hallelujah. My family never kept any records of the other families that have come and gone. So as no trouble would come to them if we were ever found out. But they're all out there somewhere, and I've got a feeling they've all found freedom at last, if not in this life, then most assuredly the next.

I hear there's trouble brewing in South Carolina. Some people think it's on account of the new president we elected. Most people, like myself, feel that it's because of slavery through and through. This town has gone North, so they say, and I'm ever glad it did. It was bound to happen anyway. Evil has to be challenged in order for good to prevail. If South Carolina secedes from the Union, so be it. For the time being, America is in God's hands–as it should be. And I have a feeling

God and our new president Mr. Lincoln will take care of us in this present storm. Something about him just screams integrity in my ears. With more men like that, we'll do all right–I reckon.

CPSIA information can be obtained at www.ICGtesting.com
Printed in the USA
BVOW040500071211

277643BV00001BA/1/P